LETTERS
TO
CUPID

D0068436

LETTERS TO CUPID

by Francess Lantz

Published by Pleasant Company Publications
Text Copyright © 2001 by Francess Lantz
Cover Illustration Copyright © 2001 by Tracy Mitchell

Visit our Web site at **americangirl.com**

Printed in the United States of America.
First Edition
02 03 04 05 06 RRD 10 9 8 7 6 5 4 3 2

The characters and events portrayed in this book are fictitious.
Any similarity to real persons, living or dead, is coincidental
and not intended by the author.

Library of Congress Cataloging-in-Publication Data
Lantz, Francess Lin, 1952–
Letters to Cupid / Francess Lantz.—1st ed.
p. cm. "AG fiction."
Summary: When thirteen-year-old Bridgette tackles the topic of "true love"
for a school report, her research gives her some insights into relationships that
help not only her own search for a boyfriend, but her parents' foundering
marriage as well.
ISBN 1-58485-375-1(hc) — ISBN 1-58485-374-3 (pbk.)
[1. Interpersonal relations—Fiction. 2. Marriage—Fiction.
3. Love —Fiction.] I. Title.
PZ7.L2947Le 2001 [FIC]—dc21 2001022774

For Cousin Carol in Pennsylvania

*With thanks to Donald Ranck of
Verdant View Farm in Paradise, Pennsylvania,
Brendan and Ryan Allison, Aurora Burd, John
Landsberg, Lou Lynda Richards, Ermila Moodley,
Steve Fraser, and Andrea Weiss*

Dear Cupid,

I'm looking for love. Mind-bending, heart-thumping, soul-stirring love. The kind you read about in romance novels. The kind you see on TV and in the movies. I'm talking sweep-you-off-your-feet, too-excited-to-sleep, Love with a capital L.

If I sound impatient, Cupid, it's because I am. You see, I'm about to turn thirteen (as of tomorrow morning at 6:23 A.M.) —an actual teenager—and, so far, life has been unbearably empty and meaningless, not to mention mind-bogglingly boring.

Come to think of it, how could it not be? I live in the world's dreariest town, with my totally uninspiring mother and father and one completely uninterest-ing seventeen-year-old brother. (Brother number two, age twenty-four, lives about two hours away.) Nothing ever happens to me. Nothing.

But with your help, Cupid, all that's going to change.

They say that when you're in love, the sky is bluer, the sun is brighter, the very air tastes sweet on your lips. A nothing town like Newley, Pennsylvania, sud-denly becomes paradise on Earth. Emily Dickinson Middle School turns into the Garden of Eden. And a plain old nobody like Bridgette Carley (that's me) blossoms into a princess in glittering glass slippers.

So bring him on—the guy who's going to send me my first love letter, take me on my first date, plant that very first kiss on my trembling lips. My Prince Charming. My knight in shining armor. My boyfriend.

And please, Cupid, send him soon.

Chapter One

"Oooh," Bridgette sighed as the credits scrolled across the TV screen, "that was so romantic!"

A hand reached in front of her and turned on the lamp. Suddenly, the sinking Titanic was just a goose-bumpy memory, and Bridgette was back in the den of her own house, safe and sound, sitting on the sofa with Jill and Cassie.

Bridgette blinked, trying to readjust to boring old reality. Not that she had anything to complain about. After all, it was her birthday, and she was spending it with her two best friends in the entire world. What more could she ask for?

She didn't have to answer the question because Cassie answered it for her.

"True love," Cassie sighed. "Wouldn't it be sweet?"

Jill nodded. "I could definitely fall for some hunky guy on a ship who wanted to draw my portrait," she said around a bite of butterscotch birthday cake. "Jack Dawson, where are you?"

Cassie hitched up her nightgown and stretched her suntanned legs across Bridgette's white, freckled ones. "Forget Jack Dawson," Cassie declared. "He's just pretend. Bring me the real Leo DiCaprio."

"Yeah, right. As if somebody like him would ever come to Newley," Jill scoffed.

Cassie shrugged. "I can dream, can't I?"

"I'm tired of dreaming," Bridgette said, hitting rewind on the remote. "I want to start living. That's why I'm setting my sights on a local boy."

"Who?" Cassie asked. Jill stopped chewing and leaned forward.

"I haven't met him yet," Bridgette admitted. "But when I do, I'll know."

"Br-r-roing!" Cassie cried, taking aim and firing an imaginary arrow. "True love!"

Bridgette nodded. "Long walks through the cornfields in the moonlight," she said, starting the girls' favorite game. They called it Love Links, a stream-of-consciousness game where they took turns listing everything they hoped true love would be.

"Slow dancing to your own special song," Jill said.

"Finding love letters in your locker," Cassie added.

"Sharing hot chocolate at the football game," said Bridgette.

"Football?" Bridgette's mother repeated, walking into the room. "I thought you girls were watching a movie."

Bridgette frowned at her mother's outfit, a stylish burnt orange pantsuit and a beige raincoat. "You're going out?"

"One of my clients just got back into town, and I promised I'd bring over the new listings. I'll only be a few minutes."

Bridgette nodded. Her mother used to be a regular old stay-at-home mom. She baked cookies, made the beds and scrubbed the toilets, volunteered as a room mother, and was always there when Bridgette got home from school. Then, two years ago, she decided to get her real estate license. Now there were dust balls under the beds, the family ate microwavable pizza for dinner, and Bridgette had to call Mom's cell phone whenever she needed to be picked up somewhere.

"Where's Dad?" Bridgette asked.

"Where do you think? He's in the garage, refinishing some junky old dresser he got at a yard sale. Now don't stay up too late, girls. And Jill, no more cake. Your mother made me promise."

Jill quickly shoved the last bite into her mouth.

Poor Jill! Bridgette thought. Her mother worked for Weight Watchers, and the whole family was on a perpetual diet. Naturally, whenever she was out of her mom's sight, Jill ate anything that wasn't nailed down.

"Can you picture any of our parents slow dancing?" Cassie asked after Bridgette's mom had left.

"Or writing each other love letters?" Jill giggled.

Bridgette sucked in her left cheek and gnawed it thoughtfully. For as long as she could remember, her mother and father had been . . . well, pretty much like everybody else's parents. They talked about what was on the calendar for the week and who was going to drive which kid where. They went out to dinner on their birthdays, their anniversary, and New Year's Eve. Occasionally, one of them gave the other a little squeeze or a peck on the cheek. They were friendly and polite and familiar. But romantic—never!

Lately, however, things were changing—and not for the better. This morning, for example, Bridgette had woken up to the sound of her parents arguing in the hallway.

"I can't pick up the cake," her mother was saying. "I have to show a house at five."

"Well, what am I supposed to do?" Dad snapped. "Put a note on the door that says, CLOSED EARLY

TO PICK UP DAUGHTER'S BIRTHDAY CAKE? That's real professional."

"Your clients would probably think it was adorable," Mom said sarcastically. "They like that warm and fuzzy stuff."

There was a pause, then Dad's voice, sounding much too laid-back, replied, "Brendan can pick up the cake on his way home from the video store. There, problem solved . . ."

"Earth to Bridgette, Earth to Bridgette," Cassie broke in, tapping on Bridgette's head. "Is there any intelligent life up there?"

Bridgette forced a laugh. "My parents have been on each other's case a lot lately. They think I haven't heard them arguing, but I have."

"Sounds like my parents every day of the week," Cassie replied. "If they don't have a screaming match at least once every twenty-four hours, they get bored."

"But your folks talk that way to *everyone*, Cassie," Jill broke in. "Mr. and Mrs. Carley are like the mom and dad on *The Brady Bunch* or something. They never raise their voices."

"Maybe they're just stressed out about the wedding," Cassie suggested. "It's only a couple of months away, right?"

Bridgette's oldest brother, Trent, was getting married in October. Her mom had been talking on the phone with the mother of Trent's fiancée practically every weekend, discussing everything from rings to rehearsal dinners. "You're probably right," Bridgette said. "Weddings always make people tense."

"Unless—" Cassie's voice trailed off.

"Unless what?" Bridgette asked anxiously.

"Nothing. I was just thinking about my Aunt Rita and Uncle Joe. They always seemed to get along great. Then, one Christmas Eve, they got into a huge fight in front of the whole family. Aunt Rita broke an angel ornament over Uncle Joe's head, and then he tossed her present into the fireplace. By New Year's Eve, they had split up."

"Come on," Jill said, laughing nervously. "No downer talk allowed. This is Bridgette's birthday, remember? Hey, let's all have another piece of cake."

"You go ahead," Bridgette said with a weak smile. Suddenly, she didn't feel hungry, not even for butterscotch birthday cake.

The sky was turning a pale pink when Bridgette opened her eyes the next morning. Cassie and Jill were still snoring softly in their sleeping bags on the floor. With a yawn, Bridgette got up and shuffled to the bathroom.

That's when she heard it. A soft rustling from the bottom of the stairs. Probably Brendan, watching another early morning movie on one of the cable channels, she decided. She tiptoed lightly down the steps and popped her head over the railing, hoping to scare him.

But it wasn't Brendan. It was Dad. He was standing next to the sofa, folding a blanket. When he saw her, he jumped.

"Bridge, you startled me." He laughed and tossed the blanket over the back of the sofa. "Happy day-after-birthday, you gorgeous teenager, you."

"What are you doing, Dad?" Bridgette asked.

"Couldn't sleep. My back is acting up. So I set up camp down here on the sofa." He stretched his arms over his head. "I'm going to make some pancakes. Wanna give me a hand?"

Bridgette shook her head, trying to ignore the sick feeling that had suddenly appeared in the pit of her stomach. "I'm going back to sleep."

She hurried to her room and crawled into her rumpled bed.

It was still warm. Pulling the covers over her head, Bridgette closed her eyes and tried to pretend she'd never gone downstairs, never seen her father, never even been awake.

Chapter Two

Eighth grade was supposed to be their best year yet. Cassie and Jill had said it would be, and Bridgette had believed it, too. Finally, they were at the top of the middle school heap. They could claim the cafeteria tables by the windows, choose electives like Photography and Web Page Design, and bask in the adoration of all the little sixth and seventh graders.

But walking to her English class on the first day of school, Bridgette didn't feel grown-up or privileged or anything even remotely special. That's because Cassie and Jill had been put in Homeroom 6, while Bridgette was in Homeroom 9. As a result, the only class the girls shared was their elective, Drama and Public Speaking.

Bridgette knew what her mom would probably say. "This is a good opportunity to make new friends. That's what I did when I got my real estate license. It's all about networking, you know."

But how can you make new friends when you've known everybody since kindergarten? Bridgette wondered. She walked into English class and looked around. Yep, same old faces, each one opening a scrapbook of memories in Bridgette's mind.

There was Melinda Wattenburg, sitting in the front row as usual—Ms. Straight A, the girl who fell off the stage at the third-grade Holiday Pageant because she refused to wear her glasses.

Behind her was Sandra Van der Hoof. No one would ever forget the time back in first grade when she peed in her pants on the slide. Especially not Allison Lu, who went down the slide after her.

Or how about Didi Sorenson, who popped Altoid mints like candy, had a race car driver for a dad, and was going out with a high-school boy who drove a dirt bike.

There were probably a dozen other girls, but nobody Bridgette would consider friend material. Besides, it wasn't a friend she was looking for. What she wanted was a boyfriend.

Bridgette took a seat next to Vaughn Steinhauser. Like all the other boys in the room, Vaughn was as familiar to her as one of her brothers.

"Hey," he said.

"Hi, Vaughn," Bridgette replied. "How was your summer?"

"Extreme. I went to San Francisco with my dad to see the Robot Wars."

"The what?"

"Robot Wars. Custom-built robots designed to destroy each other," he explained. "They go head to head in the ring, and the one left standing—or at least functioning—is the winner."

"Might be a useful addition to the football team," Bridgette said.

Vaughn laughed. It was a goofy, high-pitched snort that made people turn around in movie theaters. Whenever she heard it, she felt like gritting her teeth.

"Well, they definitely need something," Vaughn remarked. "What was their record last year? One and seven?"

Before Bridgette could answer, the bell rang and the teacher, a short, stocky woman with graying hair that looked as if it had never been combed, stepped in front of her desk and said, "Welcome, class. I'm Miss Tindall. It's going to be a very exciting year here in Room 14. Together we will sample a diverse mix of prose, poetry, and drama. We will learn to write both creative stories and critical essays."

"What does she mean *we?*" Vaughn whispered. "Shouldn't she know this stuff by now?"

Bridgette giggled.

"And best of all," Miss Tindall continued, shooting Bridgette a visual death ray, "we will each try our hand at outlining, researching, and writing some ten-page papers."

"Ten pages!" Jake Farley moaned.

"You heard me correctly," Miss Tindall replied. "Ten pages on the subject of your choice. Anything from rap music to radiology to Rembrandt. Your research options are equally limitless: the library, of course, the Internet, interviews with authorities, even personal experience."

"You mean I can research skateboarding by perfecting my ollie?" Aaron Shoening said with a smirk.

"A better example would be, if you're writing about chocolate, you might arrange to visit Hershey's Chocolate World." She patted her wild hair and smiled. "The first ten-page paper will be due on November first. Research topics must be submitted next Friday. Now, class, I'll be passing out copies of our poetry textbook. Please open to page . . ."

Bridgette and her classmates spent the rest of the period analyzing a poem by Vachel Lindsay. Daydreaming was out of the question, since Miss Tindall didn't bother waiting for people to raise their hands.

She just called on somebody, usually a boy or girl who looked lost or distracted. Those students who couldn't come up with an acceptable answer were treated to Miss Tindall's death-ray glare.

Even so, Bridgette couldn't help thinking about her research paper. What was she going to write about? Broadway musicals maybe. She loved them and had an impressive collection of soundtracks. Or maybe the Olympics. Or Impressionist art. Divorce in America?

Bridgette pictured her father, folding the blanket after his night on the sofa. As far as she knew, he hadn't slept there since. So maybe it really was his back that had been bothering him that night. On the other hand, when Bridgette tried to recall a recent conversation between her mom and dad other than an argument, she couldn't. A word here, a grunt there—that was about it. They barely even made eye contact.

The bell rang, and Bridgette was jolted back to the present. Scooping up her books, she joined the rush to the door. As the class surged into the hallway, she overheard Aaron Shoening tell Jake Farley, "Not everyone has to do a research paper, you know."

This was interesting news. Did Aaron know something she didn't? She shuffled closer. The trick was hearing Aaron over the noise.

"My brother knows a Web site . . . *(roar of the crowd)* . . . buy papers . . . *(screams, laughter)* . . . all types . . . *(roar)* . . . you bet I am . . . *(first bell)* . . . later, dude."

With every word, Bridgette's eyes grew wider and her jaw dropped, until by the time Aaron turned the corner and walked into his classroom, she looked like a hungry fish.

"Aaron Shoening is going to buy a research paper off the Web," she whispered.

Is this for real? Bridgette wondered. Or was Aaron just talking big to show off? Maybe. But if it was true, well . . . what was she going to do about it? Should she turn him in to Miss Tindall?

It was a pleasing thought. Bridgette had never liked Aaron. He wore a constant smirk on his face, and his favorite thing to say was, "Ask me if I care." Besides, back in fourth grade, Aaron had double-dog-dared her to climb to the top of the maple tree at the edge of the playground. When she did, he stood beneath her and announced to the world that her underpants were pink.

Bridgette scowled. Yes, it would feel good to get Aaron in trouble for cheating. Besides, it was the right thing to do.

But first she had to prove it was true.

Chapter Three

That evening, Bridgette was sitting at the kitchen table, reading Dear Abby and munching on tortilla chips with cheese melted on top, when her mother walked in the door.

"What are you eating?" Mom demanded. "You'll spoil your dinner."

"This *is* my dinner," Bridgette replied.

"What?" Mom spun around to look at the clock. "What time is it?"

"Six-thirty."

"You're kidding. I was just catching up on a little paperwork." She put her briefcase down on the table. "Where's Brendan? Where's your father?"

"Brendan's around somewhere. Probably in front

of the TV. I don't know where Daddy is."

"Typical." Mom opened the cabinet and noisily pulled out a pot. "Toss the nachos," she said, slamming the pot down on the stove. "I'm going to make spaghetti."

It wasn't often these days that her mother cooked, and normally Bridgette would have been thrilled. But the angry frown on Mom's face took away Bridgette's appetite.

"Scratch that," Mom said. "I'm making pasta primavera and a Caesar salad. If your father can't be bothered to show up for dinner, he'll just miss out."

She rummaged in the refrigerator for some vegetables, but all she came up with were three carrots, an onion, and some wilted celery.

"OK, make that fettuccine Alfredo. I'm pretty sure we have a jar of sauce around here somewhere." She looked at Bridgette as if she'd just noticed her. "How was school, honey?"

Bridgette shrugged. "All right, I guess. But I miss being with Cassie and Jill. And we have to write a ten-page research paper for English class."

"They're getting you ready for high school," Mom said, disappearing into the pantry. "You can see Cassie and Jill at lunch, can't you?"

"Nope. Different homerooms, different lunch periods. It stinks."

Bridgette heard a yelp from the pantry, followed by the sound of breaking glass. Mom emerged a second later, looking exasperated. "Well, so much for the Alfredo sauce." She sighed.

"I guess I'm not up to cooking tonight after all. Do you think you'll be all right with those nachos?"

"Sure, Mom."

Her mother looked relieved. "Have a carrot, hon. They're good for you."

"What's on?" Bridgette asked.

Brendan didn't bother looking up. "*It Happened One Night,*" he said.

"Mind if I watch?"

Now Brendan looked up. "Since when are you into classic movies?"

"I'm not. I just want some company."

He looked at Bridgette oddly, then motioned toward the sofa.

She sat down and gazed at the screen. A man and woman in old-fashioned clothes were standing on a country road, hitchhiking. *Bor-ing.*

How could Brendan get so excited about old movies? Bridgette wondered. He was totally obsessed with them. Well, not just old ones. If it was a movie, Brendan was interested. Old ones, new ones, even foreign ones with subtitles. In fact, he was going to

New York University next year to major in Film. He had already been accepted on early admission.

"Hey, Brendan?" she began hesitantly.

"Hmm?"

"What's up with Mom and Dad?"

He looked at her. "What do you mean?"

"Don't tell me you haven't noticed. They're barely speaking."

"Oh, that." Brendan shrugged. "They're probably freaking out about Trent's wedding. Like in *Father of the Bride*."

"You mean that Steve Martin movie?"

"No, the original—Spencer Tracy and Elizabeth Taylor. It's way better."

So Brendan blamed their parents' arguments on the wedding, too. But how could one little wedding turn Mom and Dad's marriage into a mercury-plunging freeze-out? Bridgette didn't understand.

With a sigh, she turned her attention to the TV. The man in the movie was trying to thumb a ride, but no one would stop for him. Then the woman stepped into the road and hitched up her skirt. The next car screeched to a stop.

"That's sexist," Bridgette said disapprovingly.

"Sure," Brendan replied. "But you gotta remember, this film was made in 1934. Back then, doing something like that was daring for a woman. And

Claudette Colbert's character is no wimp. She's Clark Gable's equal."

Bridgette thought it over. "So, what's this movie about anyway?"

"It's a romantic comedy. Claudette Colbert is a rich girl who just married some guy her dad hates. So Daddy whisks her away to his yacht, but she jumps overboard and heads back to her man. Clark Gable plays a reporter who's following her to get the story. Only she doesn't know he's a reporter. And then they fall in love."

Bridgette blinked. "They do? Why?"

"Because opposites attract," Brendan said as if it was the most obvious thing on earth. "Like Spencer Tracy and Katharine Hepburn in *Woman of the Year.* Or Ali MacGraw and Ryan O'Neal in *Love Story.*"

"Opposites attract, huh?" she mused. "Oh, like in *Titanic,* right? Leonardo DiCaprio's character is poor and Kate Winslet's is rich."

"Now you've got the idea," Brendan said.

"So is that the way it always works in the movies?" she asked. "Opposites fall in love?"

"Not always," he said, still gazing intently at the TV screen. "Sometimes the man and woman start off hating each other, usually because of some misunderstanding. But eventually they fall in love. That's a typical Fred Astaire–Ginger Rogers plot."

18

Bridgette couldn't believe her ears. Who would have guessed there was an expert on true love living right under her own roof? All she had to do was pick Brendan's brain about romance movies and then do whatever the women in the movies did. *Zing!* Cupid's arrow would soon be whizzing her way.

"Hold that thought, Brendan," Bridgette said, leaping up from the sofa. "I'll be right back with a pencil and a piece of paper."

Dear Cupid,

Incredible news! I've found a way to make your job easier. Thanks to my film-crazed brother, I'm going to learn how to place myself in love-friendly situations.

Brendan has made a list of movies I should watch and study. According to him, the films illustrate different proven methods for meeting Mr. Right.

1. "Opposites attract" (Boy and girl from two different worlds find each other irresistible.)

   Examples: TITANIC, WITNESS, YOU'VE GOT MAIL

2. "Meeting 'cute'" (Boy and girl meet in a cute, often quirky way. Romance follows.)

   Examples: TOP HAT, THE WEDDING PLANNER, WHILE YOU WERE SLEEPING

3. "Cat and mouse" (3 variations)

a. "Cop and criminal" (Authority figure tries to capture outlaw but instead falls in love.)

   Example: RAISING ARIZONA

b. "Detective and client" (Troubled, mysterious person seeks help.)

   Example: THE MALTESE FALCON

c. "Con artist and victim" (One person tries to scam another, and they end up head over heels.)

   Example: THE LADY EVE

4. "Cinderella story" (Person meets nerd or outcast who turns into heartthrob. Romance develops.)

   Examples: SHE'S ALL THAT, CAN'T BUY ME LOVE, PRETTY WOMAN

5. "The dangerous situation" (Danger brings two people together. Can love be far behind?)

   Examples: SPEED, CASABLANCA

Brendan says there are even more categories, but this ought to get me started.

Oh, Cupid, I'm so excited! I can't wait to start watching those movies so I can figure out who the love of my life is.

Later . . . Bad news, Cupid. Just returned from the video store, where I discovered that some of the movies Brendan told me to study are rated R. Luckily, he's promised to describe the plots for me.

Meanwhile, I rented RAISING ARIZONA, which we'll watch together tonight.

By the way, this morning at breakfast, I asked Mom and Dad how they met. He said it was at college, in anthropology class. Their seats were next to each other and they started talking.

Cupid, is it any wonder my parents aren't getting along? I mean, come on! Their story isn't anything remotely like any of the plots Brendan described.

Chapter Four

In English class the next day, Bridgette sat down beside Vaughn again, even though Miss Tindall hadn't said anything about staying in the same seats.

"Habit," she said out loud.

Vaughn turned to her. "Huh?"

"Everyone is sitting in the same seats as yesterday. We're creatures of habit, I guess."

Vaughn looked her over. "What is this?" he said at last. "Your zebra phase or something?"

"What are you talking about?" asked Bridgette.

"Yesterday you wore black pants and a white blouse. Today you're wearing a black skirt and a black-and-white-striped blouse."

Bridgette ran her fingers through her thick, red

curls. With hair that color, she was already wearing red even before she got dressed. Then, if she put on green, she looked like a Christmas decoration. Pink clashed. Yellow—Bozo the Clown. So this year, she had decided just to keep it simple. Black and white, that was it.

But she couldn't explain that to a boy. So all she did was shrug and mumble, "I like it."

Vaughn thrust his fist in the air. "Solidarity with the zebras!" he proclaimed.

"Vaughn, knock it off," she giggled.

"Don't be shy. Raise your voice and say it with me. 'Zebra lovers unite, take back the stripes!'"

Bridgette wanted to be offended, but it was just too silly. She snickered.

"Mr. Steinhauser and Ms. Carley, perhaps you didn't hear the bell ring?"

Bridgette spun around to find Miss Tindall's death-ray glare aimed at her. "No, uh, sorry," she muttered. She opened her poetry book and stole a quick glance at Vaughn. Beneath his desk, he made a fist. Bridgette felt another giggle rising up in her. Quickly, she looked away.

What she found herself looking toward was the back of Aaron Shoening's head. Suddenly, the conversation Bridgette had overheard yesterday came back to her. *My brother knows a Web site . . . buy papers . . . you bet I am.* Bridgette sucked in her left cheek. She couldn't let Aaron get away with it. But what if she was wrong? She had to have proof.

Miss Tindall was droning on about metaphors and similes, but Bridgette's thoughts slipped back to the movie she'd watched with Brendan last night, *Raising Arizona.* Nicolas Cage played a criminal who was arrested by policewoman Holly Hunter. He promised to go straight, they fell in love, and . . .

Suddenly, Bridgette was thinking about Aaron. *I'll convince him not to buy the research paper,* she decided. *He'll see the error of his ways, he'll thank me, and then—brroing!—Cupid takes over!*

OK, so maybe there were a few problems. Like, for example, she had no idea how she was going to talk Aaron out of buying the paper. Also, the two of them didn't even like each other. How were they supposed to fall in love?

It happens all the time in the movies, Bridgette reminded herself. *So why not in real life?*

She gazed at the back of Aaron's head, willing herself to find him irresistible. *Come on, Cupid,* Bridgette begged, *do your stuff.*

"Anyone sitting here?"

Aaron looked up from his lunch tray and stared at Bridgette.

"You want to sit here?" he asked.

Bridgette smiled and nodded.

"OK, I guess," he said. "But only until the guys show up."

She slid into a seat. Aaron wasn't bad-looking, really. Sleek black hair, brooding eyes. Too bad about those bushy eyebrows. *Ugh*, she thought, *they practically meet in the middle.*

She looked away. "How do you like Miss Tindall?" Bridgette asked, opening her milk carton.

Aaron shrugged.

"I think she's hard," said Bridgette. "Like making us write those research papers. Ten pages! It's going to take forever."

"Not for a brain like you," Aaron said, shoveling a bite of spaghetti into his mouth.

"I'm not a brain," Bridgette protested. "Seriously, Aaron, I'm worried. My parents are really strict. If I get anything less than a B, they'll ground me for the rest of the year."

It wasn't true, but it was part of the plan Bridgette had concocted during Math. Now, if only Aaron would bite . . .

"So? What are you telling me for?" he muttered.

Bridgette leaned across the table. "I heard you know where to buy a paper," she whispered.

Aaron squinted at her. "Who told you that?"

She leaned closer. "Do you, Aaron?"

He chewed for a while, ignoring her. Finally, he said, "You got any money?"

She nodded. "I baby-sat all summer."

"Meet me at the bike rack after school." Then he picked up his tray and walked to another table.

Bridgette smiled. Soon she'd be alone with Aaron, begging him to give up his evil ways, convincing him that with her help, he could become a good person. And then he'd look into her eyes, take her in his arms . . .

The thought of kissing Aaron made her stomach turn over. *But then,* she reminded herself, *isn't that how you're supposed to feel when you're in love?*

When the last bell rang, Bridgette practically ran to the bike rack. By the time she got there, her heart was pounding. *It's because I'm meeting Aaron,* she told herself.

She thought about his dark, brooding eyes (without the eyebrows). There was a lot more to Aaron than most people realized, she was sure of it.

"Did you ride your bike?" he asked as he walked up to her.

She shook her head. "I took the bus."

He looked annoyed. "Get on," he ordered.

She climbed on his bike. He straddled the frame

in front of her and pedaled standing up. When they turned corners, she had to grab his waist to keep from falling off. But if Aaron liked having her arms around him, he didn't show it.

They pulled up in front of his house and she followed him inside. His toddler sister was there with a baby-sitter.

"Come on," he said, leading Bridgette into the family room and shutting the door.

He turned on the computer and connected to the Internet. Soon he was clicking from Web page to Web page, moving so quickly she couldn't memorize the sequence. Finally, he stopped at a page with an alphabetical listing of subject headings.

"Pick a subject, any subject," he said with a grin.

"Um, what are you picking?" she asked.

"Internet fraud," he smirked. "Check it out."

He clicked on the subject heading, then typed in "middle-school version." Instantly, a research paper appeared on the screen. "All I have to do is type in my name and print it out." He sat back in the chair and crossed his arms. "Your turn, Bridgette. What's your favorite subject?"

"I'm not going to cheat," she said.

"Wha—" he began.

"You don't have to either." She reached out and took his hand. "I know you're a good person, Aaron.

That is, you could be, if you had somebody who believed in you. You're smart. You can write your own paper."

"What are you talking about?" he asked.

"I'll help you. We'll write it together. It'll be fun."

She pictured intimate afternoons in the public library, their heads bent together over a book. Then long walks around the duck pond, hand in hand.

He looked at her, then down at her hand that was still holding his. Slowly, his face broke into a thin smile. "Let me get this straight," he said. "You're offering to help me write my research paper?"

"Yes," she said. "Of course. If it means you won't cheat."

"It's a deal," he replied, slipping his hand away. "If you promise to help me, I promise I won't buy a paper off the Internet."

Bridgette felt like laughing for joy. Her plan had worked! She had convinced Aaron to go straight.

She gazed dreamily into his dark brown eyes. Could true love be far behind?

Chapter Five

It was a long walk home, and Aaron didn't offer to take her on his bike. But Bridgette didn't mind. It gave her time to think. She strolled down the road, past farm fields crowded with fat orange pumpkins. *Someday soon,* she thought, *I'll be walking these roads hand in hand with Aaron.*

A horse-drawn buggy clattered past Bridgette, with an Amish farmer at the reins. Downtown, near her father's antique shop, tourists lined up for buggy rides—twenty dollars for a half hour.

Normally, Bridgette wouldn't be caught dead near a tourist trap like that. But today, imagining herself riding in the back of a buggy with Aaron, it all seemed unspeakably romantic.

"True love," she breathed. She hadn't admitted it to Aaron, but *that* was her favorite topic.

So why not write her research paper about it? She already had a list of movies she was planning to watch. She could read books on the subject, too. Maybe she could even interview couples who were in love. And as for the personal experience part, well, that was where Aaron came in.

Bridgette walked faster, thinking about all the questions she would finally have the answers to. Like how to tell the difference between true love and a crush. The pluses and minuses of playing hard to get. And how to keep love alive through the years.

That last question was an important one. If she could learn the answer, she might be able to understand what was going on with her mother and father. She might even be able to make it better.

The house was empty when Bridgette got home. She tossed off her jacket and hit the play button on the answering machine.

"Josie, it's me." It was Dad's voice. "I'm stopping by the lawyer's office after work tonight. Don't hold dinner for me. I'll get something on the way."

A lawyer? Why was her dad seeing a lawyer? The word "divorce" popped into Bridgette's head, and a queasy feeling wafted over her.

No, she told herself, *it couldn't be that. It just couldn't be.*

She wandered through the house, wishing that Brendan were there. They'd rent *Father of the Bride,* the original version, and reassure themselves that their parents' bizarre behavior was just a phase.

But Brendan was at his job at the video store. So Bridgette picked up the phone and called Cassie, eager to dish about her close encounter with Aaron. But Cassie wasn't home, and neither was Jill.

"I have to talk to someone or I'll burst!" she said out loud.

Just then, the telephone rang. Bridgette leaped for it, hoping to hear Jill or Cassie on the other end.

"Hello, honey," Bridgette's grandmother said.

"Oh, hi, Grams," Bridgette answered, trying not to let disappointment creep into her voice.

"How's school going?" Grams asked.

Bridgette paused, thinking about Aaron and their research papers. Soon she and Aaron would be working on them together. "Grams," she confided, "I think I'm falling in love."

"Ah, first love," her grandmother said warmly. "I remember it well."

"With Grandpa, you mean?" Bridgette asked.

"Oh, heavens, no. I had quite a few boyfriends before I found my true love."

True love. Suddenly, an idea popped into Bridgette's head. "Grams, can I interview you for my school research paper? I'm writing about true love."

"Well . . . that sounds a little personal. Who's going to read this paper?"

"Just my teacher and, uh, maybe the kids in my class," Bridgette admitted.

"Oh, my," Grams said. "I don't think I'd feel comfortable with that. In any case, everything I know about love can be summed up in two sentences. Love is like a rose bush. If you want the flowers, you have to get poked by a few thorns."

"That's it?" Bridgette asked, perplexed. "But what about romance? And what happens when you fight? How do you handle that?"

"You'll understand when you're older."

"But Grams—"

"Is your mother there, sweetie?"

"She's at work," Bridgette said. "Listen, can I interview Grandpa for my research paper?"

"About romance?" Grams laughed uncomfortably. "Maybe you should just go to the library and check out some books. That's how we did research in my day."

"But—"

"Tell your mother to call me when she gets in. Don't forget, dear."

Bridgette hung up the phone. It was obvious that she wasn't going to get any useful information out of Grams or Grandpa.

Who else could she interview? Mom? Dad? The neighbors? But what if they all decided her questions were too personal?

The phone rang again. Bridgette grabbed it, certain it was Jill or Cassie this time. Instead, a man asked, "Are you paying too much for your long distance service?"

With a groan, Bridgette slammed down the telephone. Then, suddenly, she remembered a call she'd gotten last month. A consumer research company had been collecting information about teen buying habits. The caller had asked Bridgette a series of questions about her likes and dislikes. Then, as a way of saying thanks, the company had sent her a booklet of discount coupons for shampoo, makeup, and breath mints.

"That's it!" Bridgette cried.

All she had to do was call people and pretend to be from a research company. She could say she was collecting information for an important study about relationships in today's society. If someone agreed to answer her questions, she'd assure the person that the information would be used for research purposes only. Then she'd promise to send some coupons. She didn't have a whole booklet of them, but she could cut out a few from the newspaper.

There was only one problem. Everyone would know by her voice that she was a kid. No one would take her seriously.

Unless . . .

She ran into the laundry room and rummaged through the recycling bin until she found the newspaper from last Sunday. Just as she thought, there was an advertisement for the Electronics Barn that showed a picture of something called a Voicetech Voice Changer. "No bigger than a telephone answering machine. Just plug it into your phone and transform your voice into male or female, young or old. Only $19.99."

Twenty dollars! She'd saved lots more than that from baby-sitting. With a smile, she folded the newspaper under her arm and hurried to her room.

Chapter Six

Aaron was waiting for Bridgette at her locker the next morning. When she saw him, her heart did a tap dance against her ribs.

"Hi, Aaron," she breathed.

"Hey. Wanna eat lunch with me later?" he asked.

She felt like shouting her answer to the rooftops, but she restrained herself. She didn't want to do anything to embarrass Aaron. "Yes," Bridgette said. "I'd like that."

He nodded and walked away.

In English class, Bridgette handed in her research paper topic. "Hmmm," Miss Tindall mused as she glanced at Bridgette's paper. "Interesting. Just how much personal research do you plan to do?"

Bridgette blushed and shot a quick glance at Aaron, who was snickering about something with Jake Farley. "It all depends."

Miss Tindall smiled knowingly, as if she'd actually had some experience with love. "I'll read your paper with interest," she said.

"Aaron Shoening?" Cassie gasped, turning from her open locker. "But he's a total idiot!"

"Oh, he just acts that way so he won't get hurt," Bridgette explained. "Inside, he's very sensitive. You should have seen his face when I said I'd help him with his paper. He was so grateful."

"Really?" Cassie said uncertainly.

"Just wait. Pretty soon you won't recognize Aaron. My love is going to turn him into a new person. A better person."

"Sounds like a TV commercial," Cassie said. "Get the new and improved Aaron Shoening. On sale now!"

Bridgette smiled sympathetically. Cassie didn't understand boys like she did. But then, Cassie also didn't have a movie expert brother like Brendan to teach her.

"Wait and see," was all Bridgette said.

♥

Vaughn was standing by the cafeteria door. When he saw her, he raised a hand in greeting.

Bridgette pretended she hadn't seen him. She didn't want to talk to Vaughn right now. She was looking for Aaron. But Vaughn stepped in front of her, blocking her way. "There's something I think you should know," he said.

"What?"

"Aaron's been bragging to his friends about how you're going to write his research paper for him."

Bridgette laughed. "I think you misunderstood. I said I would help him. We're going to work on our papers together."

"That's not what Aaron is telling people," Vaughn said. "I overheard him in P.E. talking to Roger Torres and Todd Lutz. He was telling them how you think you're saving him from cheating."

"But I am," Bridgette insisted.

"Bridgette, they were laughing about how completely clueless you are."

She felt her face grow hot. "That's a lie!" she cried.

Vaughn didn't argue. "I just thought I should tell you," he said. Then he turned and disappeared into the crowd.

Bridgette stood in the doorway, letting the people stream by her. She didn't want to believe Vaughn, but what reason would he have to lie to her?

Bridgette forced herself to enter the cafeteria. She saw Aaron waving to her. Reluctantly, she walked over and sat down.

"Hey," he said. "Aren't you buying lunch?"

"I'm not hungry."

"How come?"

She took a deep breath. "Aaron, I'm not going to write your research paper for you."

"What are you talking about?" he asked.

"I know you've been telling your friends that I am. But I'm not going to. That would be just as wrong as buying a paper off the Internet."

"I don't know what you've heard," Aaron said indignantly, "but it's not true. I don't want you to cheat. In fact, I know you wouldn't. You're too good a person, Bridgette."

She felt her heart skitter. For one brief moment, she pictured the two of them standing together in the library stacks. In her imagination, they were so close she could smell his shampoo. They spotted the book they needed, and both of them reached for it at the same time. Their hands touched and . . .

"Did I tell you I'm going to be playing ice hockey on the YMCA team this winter?" he asked.

"No."

"I want you to come watch me, Bridgette. Will you do that?"

"OK," she sighed. She imagined herself sitting in the front row of the hockey rink, cheering as Aaron made a goal.

Aaron took a sip of his milk. "With all the practices and stuff, I'm going to be busy," he said. "Really busy. So Bridgette, I need you to help me with my research like you promised. Nothing major. Just find a few articles. Then take some notes and—"

Now Bridgette came crashing down to the cold, hard ice. Aaron was trying to con her into doing his work for him.

Con. Suddenly Bridgette realized that she and Aaron weren't playing cop and criminal anymore. Now Aaron was being the con artist and she was his victim, just like in *The Lady Eve.* She hadn't seen that movie yet, but Brendan had told her a little about it. Barbara Stanwyck played a card shark who tried to con a clueless scientist played by Henry Fonda.

But what happens when the victim figures out he's being conned? Bridgette wondered. She wished she could call Brendan and ask him. But there was no time for that now. She'd just have to rely on her instincts.

"You're a bright guy, Aaron," she said. "If you used your intelligence to do your own work instead of trying to con people into doing it for you, you'd be a straight-A student."

"I'm not trying to con you," he said, giving her an "I'm insulted" look. "All I'm asking for is a little help. Won't you help me, Bridgette?"

"No," she said. "I'm sorry to disappoint you, but it just wouldn't be right."

Aaron leaned back in his chair and crossed his arms over his chest. "OK, then, I guess I'll be using that Web site after all," he said with a smirk.

"Oh, Aaron, no," Bridgette begged. "Promise me you won't."

"The only promise I'm making is that I'm acing that research paper. Wait and see."

Wait and see. Just a few minutes earlier, Bridgette had been saying those same words to Cassie. She'd been so confident then. Now, however, it looked like Cupid was about to take a nosedive.

But what had Bridgette expected? That Aaron would gaze into her baby blues and instantly see the error of his ways? *Come on, Bridgette,* she told herself. *The happy ending doesn't happen in the first half hour of the movie. There have to be a few twists and turns along the way.*

And then she thought of a twist that would really get things moving.

She would turn Aaron in for cheating.

Oh, he'd be mad at first. Furious, even. But that's how tough love worked. In the end, Aaron would realize that she was only trying to help him. And he'd thank her for it—by falling madly in love with her.

Aaron was still smirking at her. She smiled back—a warm, tender smile that she hoped conveyed her deep feelings toward him. "I have to go now," she said, standing up and pushing in her chair. "Whatever happens, please remember that I have your best interests at heart."

"Ask me if I care," he called as she walked away.

Chapter Seven

"I hope you're happy, you stupid Girl Scout," Aaron said, falling into step beside Bridgette on the way into homeroom the next morning. "Tindall called my parents. They closed my Internet account and grounded me for the rest of the month."

"I'm not happy at all," Bridgette said, and she meant it. "I didn't want to hurt you. I just wanted you to do the right thing."

"Oh, I see," he said with mock earnestness. "I guess I'm supposed to thank you."

Someday you will, she thought, picturing the closing scene of *The Lady Eve.* She'd watched it last night with Brendan. Barbara Stanwyck looks into Henry Fonda's eyes and says, "Don't you know I've waited all my life for you?" Then he takes her in his arms and kisses her.

That will be us, Bridgette told herself.

"I'll get you back for this, you little brownnose," Aaron muttered. Then he turned and marched away.

Bridgette pushed open the girls' locker room door and walked into the high-school swimming center. She was greeted by the familiar smell of chlorine.

"Hey, there, Bridgette," called Mr. Lafayette, the swim coach, his deep voice echoing off the high ceiling. "Ready to get wet?"

"Definitely," she replied. She loved to swim, anywhere, anytime. But after her run-in with Aaron, she was especially eager to lose herself in the repetitive motion of endless laps.

"Check out the pool," Mr. Lafayette said. "They finally painted it this summer."

When Bridgette gazed down the lane lines, she noticed something else—or rather, someone else. It was Vaughn, crouching at the edge of the deep end, cleaning out one of the filter baskets. She walked over and asked, "What are you doing here?"

Vaughn plucked a wad of hair and gum out of the basket and looked up. "Hi, Bridgette. I'm working here now, three afternoons a week. Pool maintenance. It's a very glamorous job, as you can see."

Bridgette giggled. Then she said, "You were right about Aaron."

"Yeah."

The shrill squeal of Mr. Lafayette's whistle cut through the warm air. "Middle-school swimmers," he called, "into the pool!"

"Gotta go," Bridgette said. "But I wanted to say thanks for setting me straight. I think it's going to make my relationship with Aaron a lot stronger."

Vaughn looked at her quizzically, but all he said was, "Have a good swim."

When practice ended, Bridgette walked over to her father's antique shop. She liked hanging out there better than taking the bus home to an empty house. Usually, she did her homework while Dad helped customers or finished up paperwork. Then they drove home together.

Bridgette walked past Honest Abel's All-You-Can-Eat Family Restaurant. As usual, the parking lot was crowded with cars. She crossed the street to her father's shop. Through the bay windows, beyond the inviting jumble of furniture and quilts, she could see her father chatting with a customer.

Bridgette threw open the door, making the little iron bell over her head tinkle merrily. Dad looked up and smiled, then went back to his conversation.

Bridgette wandered around, checking out the antiques Dad had collected since her last visit. She was admiring a pair of cornhusk dolls when a flash of black outside the window caught her eye.

A horse and wagon pulled in next to Honest Abel's. A teenage boy got out and tied up the horses. Bridgette had noticed the boy many times over the years, delivering fresh produce to the restaurant with his parents.

"How was swim practice?" Dad asked.

Bridgette turned around. The customer was gone, and Dad was smiling at her. He looked a little tired. His hair—once as thick and red as Bridgette's, but now thinning and going white at the temples—needed a trim.

"It was good. Where's Suzie?" Bridgette asked. Suzie was Dad's assistant manager.

"She quit," Dad said.

"You're kidding. Why?" Suzie had worked with Dad since before Bridgette joined the swim team, before Trent went away to college, before . . . well, since forever.

"It was just time for her to move on," Dad said vaguely. He picked up a candlestick and polished it with his sleeve. "I don't know what I'm going to do without her. The antiques business is all about building relationships. Not the kind of relationships you make in *real estate.*" He said "real estate" as if it were dog doo. "Those last about as long as your average rock 'n' roll song. But I'm talking about lifetime connections. Your mother doesn't understand that."

"What does that have to do with Suzie?" Bridgette asked.

"Everything. Suzie knew this store and our customers as well as I did. Maybe even better. We were a team."

Bridgette wasn't sure what her father was talking about. It almost sounded as if he was comparing Suzie to Mom, and Suzie was coming out on top. Bridgette looked out the window, anxious to think about something else.

Across the street, the Amish boy was unloading a basket of squash from the back of the wagon. She'd never noticed before, but he was tall and kind of good-looking. She watched the easy way he hoisted the basket onto his shoulder. *I bet he's got major muscles,* Bridgette thought.

The movie *Witness,* which Brendan had rented the night before, popped into Bridgette's head. Kelly McGillis played an Amish woman who falls in love with a police detective, played by Harrison Ford, who's investigating a murder.

What would it be like to be Amish? Bridgette wondered. *Maybe not all that bad,* she decided, *if someone like Harrison Ford was in love with you!*

She watched the boy stroll into the restaurant. "Opposites attract," she mumbled.

"What?" Dad asked.

"Nothing. Are you almost ready to go?"

Dad let out a long, slow sigh. Then he nodded and grabbed his keys. He was halfway to the door when he stopped and put his hands on his hips. "Bridgette, how would you like to go to Honest Abel's for dinner?"

"Sure," she answered. Her mouth watered as she pictured the long buffet table heaped with Amish food. "What about Mom and Brendan?" she asked. "Do you want me to call and tell them to meet us?"

"Oh, don't bother," her dad said, throwing open the door. "Brendan will microwave a pizza the way he always does. And your mother—" the iron bell jangled harshly as they stepped outside "—she'll probably be working late anyway."

Chapter Eight

Bridgette's father locked the shop, and together they crossed the street.

The Amish boy was still there, chatting with a plump woman at the restaurant's kitchen door. His black, wide-brimmed hat was about as far from hip as you could possibly get. Still, Bridgette decided, it looked pretty good on him. And the hair that stuck out beneath it was thick and blond and wavy.

"Dermott, hello!" a man with a white handlebar mustache called to Bridgette's father from across the parking lot.

"Harold, how have you been?" Dad asked as the man approached. They shook hands.

"Marvelous. Say, I didn't see your booth at the

antiques fair this summer. What happened?"

"Not enough money in it. I'm thinking of opening a shop in Philadelphia. That's where all the real collectors are."

Bridgette kicked a pebble with her toe. It looked as if the men were settling in for a long talk. She glanced over at the Amish boy. He was tipping his hat to the woman, getting ready to leave.

Slowly, quietly, she inched away and strolled casually toward the horse and wagon, wondering if there was any way she could start up a conversation. She tried out a few opening sentences in her head.

Excuse me, do you realize you're parked in a No Horse zone?

Nice hat. Did you buy it around here?

Hey, babe, I've been admiring your squash.

But wait, what was she doing? She was in love with Aaron, and he was in love with her—or at least he would be after he finally saw the error of his ways and realized he had her to thank for leading him down the path of righteousness.

The Amish boy was climbing into the wagon now. In another moment, he'd be gone. Out of Bridgette's life forever—well, until the next time he delivered vegetables to Abel's, anyway.

"Is your horse friendly?" she blurted out.

The boy spun around with an alarmed expression

on his face. Then he quickly stared down at his boots. "Guess so," he muttered.

Gathering up her courage, she took a step closer. "Can I pet him?"

"Guess so," he said again.

She reached out her hand. The horse shook its head and gave a fierce snort. Bridgette jumped back with a gasp.

"He isn't much used to strangers," the boy said. There was an uncomfortable pause. "Nor am I," he added.

Bridgette suddenly flashed back to a scene in *Witness*. Harrison Ford and Kelly McGillis were in the barn, and he turned on his car radio. The tension grew as he took her in his arms and led her in a forbidden dance. Then, as the music faded, they paused, staring deeply into each other's eyes, and . . .

"Giddyup," the boy clucked, taking up the reins.

"Wait," Bridgette called out. "We don't have to be strangers. My name is Bridgette Carley. What's yours?"

The boy pulled back on the reins. He squinted down at Bridgette, as if deciding whether he should tell her. "Jacob Yoder," he said at last.

Then he tipped his hat and gave the reins a shake. "Good evening to you," he said as the horse clopped slowly across the parking lot.

"Good evening to you," Bridgette called, waving after him. "See you soon."

"Who was that?"

Bridgette looked up to find her father standing beside her.

"Jacob," she said, savoring the sound of the word as it rolled off her lips. "Jacob Yoder. We just met."

She walked with her father across the parking lot. "Don't you think it's weird," she remarked, "that we live so close to Amish people, we ride by them on the road, we buy vegetables at their farm stands—but we don't even know them?"

"They live in our world, but apart from it," Dad pointed out. "That's a basic tenet of their religion."

"Well, sure," Bridgette replied, "but that doesn't mean we can't be friendly. And it might be kind of nice to live like they do, don't you think? No computers, no answering machines, no telephones. Just a man and a woman, working side by side, surviving off the land."

"I'd like to see you live without a telephone," Dad said as they walked into the restaurant. "Mmm, smell that food! I'd better loosen my belt a couple of notches."

Soon they were circling the buffet table, heaping their plates with broasted chicken, pork sausage, corn, squash, and buttered noodles.

"I just love AY-mish food," Dad said loudly as they took a seat at one of the long, crowded tables.

"Dad," Bridgette giggled. "Stop!" Her father loved to imitate the tourists who visited their town. His impressions were always funny, and always horribly embarrassing.

"What's this?" Dad drawled to a passing waitress.

"That's sauerkraut, sir," she explained patiently.

"You don't say," he remarked. "What's it made from? Looks like worms or something."

"It's cabbage." The waitress shot Dad a look and quickly walked away.

Bridgette squealed, "Dad! You're awful!"

"Can't help myself. Being with my one and only daughter just puts me in a jolly mood."

Bridgette smiled. It felt good to be alone with her father. Still, she wished he would stop joking around for a minute. Maybe then she could ask him what was going on between him and her mother. If she could even figure out how to phrase the question.

"Um," Bridgette finally began, "I was wondering, Dad . . . are things OK with you and Mom?"

"Things?" Dad repeated.

"Well . . . like that night you slept on the sofa."

He chuckled nervously, then pushed back his chair and jumped to his feet. "I'm ready for seconds. How about you?"

It was almost seven o'clock when they pulled into the driveway. Mom was waiting for them at the back door, arms folded and lips pressed tightly together. "Where have you been?" she demanded. "I expected you home an hour ago. Dinner's stone cold!"

"Don't tell me you actually *made* dinner," Dad said to her.

"Don't be smart," Mom snapped. "I was worried sick. Where were you?"

"We went to Abel's," Bridgette explained. "I guess we should have called."

"That was your father's responsibility," Mom said. Then she added under her breath, "Of course, responsibility isn't exactly one of his strong points."

"Don't start, Josephine," Dad warned.

Bridgette's stomach was clenched as tightly as her parents' jaws. *Stop it, stop it, stop it!* she wanted to scream at them. Instead, she muttered, "I'm going upstairs," and hurried out of the room.

She closed the door to her bedroom and flopped down on the bed. She could still hear the tenseness in her parents' voices, even muffled through the floorboards. Bridgette shut her eyes and thought about Jacob. She'd studied the Amish in school. They were modest, polite, and peace-loving. She bet Jacob's mom and dad never fought like this.

Downstairs, a door slammed. Bridgette opened her eyes and found herself looking at the Voicetech Voice Changer she'd bought at the Electronics Barn last night. Beside it was an adapter that would allow her to tape-record her conversations.

Both devices were still in their boxes. Now she sat up and opened the packages.

The instructions seemed simple enough. She connected a few cables, plugged in the cord, and turned the voice-changer pitch setting to LOW.

Quickly, before she could change her mind, she picked up the phone and punched in seven random numbers. Two rings later, a woman's voice answered.

Bridgette gulped. Could she pull this off?

"Hello?" the voice said. "Is anyone there?"

"Yes . . . uh, good evening," Bridgette stammered. "This is, um, the Carley Institute for Sociological Research. Do you have a moment to answer a few questions?"

TRANSCRIPT OF INTERVIEW #1

Subject: Female, age 38, married with two children, part-time bookkeeper at a doctor's office

Q: How long have you been married?
A: It'll be ten years this March.

Q: How did you and your husband meet?
A: That's a funny story. I was the public relations director at a hospital--this was back when I worked full-time and had a career, not just a job. Anyway, I interviewed Jim for a position. Right off the bat, I liked him. He was so nervous, he kept popping breath mints and crossing and uncrossing his legs. It was so endearing. And the way his hair curled around his ears. I loved that. But I couldn't hire him.

Q: Why not?
A: He didn't have the qualifications. Then, about a month later, we ran into each other at Sears and he asked me out. I didn't know this at the time, but apparently he just wanted to get back at me for not hiring him. He was planning the worst possible date--dinner at McDonald's and a moonlight stroll by the town dump! But we started talking over Big Macs, and one thing led to another.

Q: True love?
A: True love. (laughter) Sometimes that's hard to remember when I'm making dinner and the kids are screaming and Jim is walking around in sweats and slippers. But yeah, I guess it is.

Q: What do you do to keep love alive?
A: (pause) We try to go out to a movie every couple of weeks, just the two of us. If we can get a sitter. But maybe the best part is just lying around on Sunday mornings, with the kids between us and Barney on TV. We talk, giggle, nap. It's great!

Q: But I mean, what do you do that's romantic?
A: Romance? What's that? (laughter) No, seriously, Jim can be very romantic. For my birthday he brought me flowers. And sometimes he just comes up behind me and gives me a hug for no reason. But it's not like it used to be, before the kids came. We just don't have the time anymore. Or the energy.

Q: So that's a problem.
A: Well, it's different, definitely. But in some ways, it's better. Jim and I and the kids, we're a family. You know what I mean?

Dear Cupid,

I'm so confused. Aaron Shoening is supposed to be falling in love with me. So why does he stick his finger down his throat and pretend to gag every time I look his way? And why can't I get Jacob Yoder out of my mind? His hair is the same color as a bale of hay stacked in an Amish barn. And his eyes are like dark, moist soil.

That sounds like I'm saying his eyes look like mud, which they don't. More like potting soil. Or chocolate pudding. Or something. All I know is, they kill me.

Maybe I'll go back to Honest Abel's on Monday and see if Jacob shows up. Who am I kidding? Of course I will. The instant swim practice ends, I'll sprint to the parking lot of the restaurant. I won't even stop at Dad's shop.

Speaking of Dad, he and Mom are no longer fighting. Instead, they're giving each other the cold shoulder. When they pass each other in the hall, I can almost see the freezer burn forming on their lips.

Cupid, love is so baffling. Last night, I conducted my first telephone interview. The voice changer worked great. So great, in fact, that the woman I was interviewing called me "sir." She was eager to talk, too, and at first I thought I was going to get some useful information. But it turned out she knew less about love than I do.

I mean, the woman's working at a dead-end job, then rushing home to take care of her husband and two screaming kids. She's lucky if she has time to brush her teeth. And yet she acted as if it was all perfectly normal. Nice, even.

If that's what happens to a marriage after a few years, it's no wonder Mom and Dad are at each other's throats. Maybe the trick is not to have kids. Not buy a house. Maybe not even get married in the first place.

Like in WITNESS. In the movie, Harrison Ford and Kelly McGillis are in love, but deep down they know they'll never be together. That's what makes their relationship so painful, yet so unbelievably hot!

Just like Jacob and me. Not that we have a relationship yet, not really. But after Monday, who knows?

I'm doing my part, Cupid. Now come on, do yours.

Chapter Nine

When Bridgette heard the clip-clop of the horse's hooves, her heart responded with a little clip-clop of its own.

Suddenly, Jacob's head and shoulders appeared over the rise in the road. The sun was behind him, creating a halo effect around his head. Just like an angel, Bridgette thought. As the horse and cart moved over the hill and down the other side toward her, Bridgette had to will herself not to run forward to meet him.

She thought about the scene in *Witness* when Kelly McGillis takes off her Amish bonnet and runs out to embrace Harrison Ford. She can't deny her attraction any longer, can't continue to hide it. So she throws herself into Harrison's waiting arms.

The wagon rolled right past Bridgette into Abel's parking lot. Jacob didn't even look up. Of course, she quickly reminded herself, he was probably concentrating on the traffic.

"Hi, Jacob!" she called, jogging after him. "What did you bring today?"

He squinted down at her as if he'd never laid eyes on her before. "Bridgette Carley," he said at last.

She beamed. "You remembered."

"I have squash, cabbage, and pumpkins," he said, climbing down from the wagon. "What would you like to buy?"

"Buy? Oh, uh, I'm not here to buy anything."

Jacob looked confused. She wanted to tell him she was there to see him, only him. But what if she scared him away? Best to go slow, she decided.

"I, uh, I'm writing a research paper for school on Amish farming," she said. "I was wondering if I could ask you a few questions?"

Jacob considered a moment. "Yes, I suppose," he answered. "But first I must make my delivery."

"Let me help," Bridgette said, throwing her arms around a basket of cabbage and heaving it toward herself.

Yikes, it was heavy! Fortunately, Jacob appeared at her side and grabbed it before it fell. As he did, his shoulder shoved against hers, and his forearm brushed her cheek. She turned to him, breathing in the fresh smell of . . . manure?

He was gone before she could get much of a whiff. Maybe it was just dirt, she told herself.

She leaned against the wagon and watched with awe as he unloaded the produce effortlessly. "You're strong," she said.

"I like to work," he replied simply.

"You sure are different from the boys I know. The only time they break a sweat is when they're tapping the controls of a video game."

He didn't answer, just went on carrying baskets of produce into the kitchen. Finally, when he was finished, he walked over to her and said, "What did you want to ask me?"

Bridgette's mind went into overdrive. What should she ask him? If he would take off his hat so she could admire his curls? Take her walking through moonlit fields of Indian corn? Share bites of shoo-fly pie with her behind the barn?

"So, uh, you don't use electricity on your farm, right?" she asked.

"That's true."

"It sounds so . . . old-fashioned." She didn't mean it as a put-down. In fact, the idea of eating by candlelight every evening was a very pleasing thought.

"We use a diesel-powered engine to pump corn silage into the silo," he said, pulling her back to the here and now. "And pneumatic and hydraulic systems with self-starting diesel engines for many other purposes."

"Oh. No kidding." She gazed at his soft lips and wondered what he looked like when he smiled. "I'd love to see your farm," she said. "Would you give me a tour?"

"You're welcome to visit us."

"Thanks!" she exclaimed. "How about now?"

His eyes widened in alarm—or was it anticipation? "Now?" he asked.

"I'd love to ride along with you," she said. "Why not? Please?"

"Well . . ." He smiled awkwardly (it was an even more adorable smile than she'd imagined) and held out his hand to help her into the wagon. As their fingers touched, her skin tingled.

And then she was sitting beside him, and they were riding together out of the parking lot. Now it was her rear end that was tingling, not to mention rocking and bouncing repeatedly against the seat.

"Ouch!" Bridgette cried, grabbing the front of the wagon as the horse broke into a trot.

Jacob laughed. "This is your first time in a horse-drawn wagon, yes?"

"Yes!" she gasped.

He jiggled the reins and the horse went faster. Bridgette held on tightly. It was too noisy to talk, too frightening to do anything else.

Soon they had left the town and were moving past fields of soybeans, Indian corn, and pumpkins. Jacob stared at the road ahead, looking serious as the wagon clattered and the cars roared by.

Finally he turned the wagon down a long gravel driveway. To the left stood a modest wooden farmhouse. To the right was a white barn and a muddy enclosure crowded with cows. Beside it was something that looked like a swimming pool, except it was filled with brown, liquidy goo.

"What's that?" Bridgette asked, pointing.

"The manure tank," he said.

A second later, the smell hit her and she knew for certain that the odor she had sniffed on Jacob was indeed manure. *Ugh!*

"Sarah!" Jacob called out suddenly. His face broke into a broad smile.

An Amish teenage girl was standing on the porch of the farmhouse, holding a basket. "Good afternoon, Jacob," she replied. She eyed Bridgette quizzically.

Jacob stopped the wagon and jumped down. This time he didn't hold out his hand for Bridgette. She stepped down on wobbly legs.

"Sarah, this is Bridgette Carley," he told the girl. "She's writing a report on Amish farming. Bridgette, this is our neighbor, Sarah Zook."

"Good afternoon," Sarah said. Then she turned back to Jacob and asked him a question in what sounded like German. They both chuckled at some private joke.

Bridgette smiled uncomfortably. "Can you show me the barn?" she asked.

"Yes, gladly," Jacob said. "Come."

They walked through a side door, with Sarah following behind. The smell of manure filled Bridgette's nostrils.

"This is where we milk the cows," Jacob explained. "And over here, we keep the calves."

"Oh, they're sweet!" Bridgette exclaimed.

Jacob said something to Sarah in German again, and she giggled.

She likes him, Bridgette thought irritably.

Jacob led Bridgette outside to a row of troughs. "This is where we feed the cows." Five cows, looking considerably larger than any cow had ever looked from the Carley family car, mooed loudly and lined up at the troughs hoping for dinner.

Bridgette glanced at Jacob and Sarah. They were talking in German again. Bridgette scowled. Somehow she had to make Jacob see that she was the one he should be paying attention to. Like Harrison Ford's character, she would prove she could handle herself on an Amish farm.

"Nice looking cows," she remarked casually, walking over and giving the closest one a hearty pat on the rump. "I'll bet—"

The startled cow jerked sideways and gave a kick. Bridgette screamed and stumbled backward, her arms rotating like propellers, until gravity finally took over.

She landed with a thud in a moist cow patty.

Jacob and Sarah laughed so hard that tears came to their eyes. Then Jacob held out his hand and asked, "Perhaps now you would like to see where we keep the pigs?"

TRANSCRIPT OF INTERVIEW #2

Subject: Female, age 29, unmarried, manicurist at a nail salon

Q: Do you have a boyfriend?
A: (giggling) Yes.

Q: How long have you been together?
A: It seems like forever.

Q: How did you meet?
A: It was love at first sight. I took one look at that handsome face and said, "This is the one."

Q: What makes him so special?
A: He's good-looking, smart, sensitive. And talented! He's in the Air Force and flies fighter jets. He's also a race car driver. And he can beat pretty much anyone at pool.

Q: Really? He sounds awesome. Is he romantic, too?
A: Is he ever! He's always surprising me with little gifts, or bringing me flowers. He even writes poems about me.

Q: Do you ever fight?
A: How could we when we can practically read each other's minds? It's almost like we're two halves of the same person. (long sigh) He completes me.

Q: Gosh, that sounds amazing. Are you planning to get married?

A: Of course! Now that he's dumped that bimbo Nicole, it's just a matter of time.

Q: Nicole?

A: Kidman. Honestly, I don't know what Tom saw in her.

Q: Tom? You mean Tom Cruise?

A: It was hard for him to leave her because of the kids. I understand that. Tom's a doting father, you know.

Q: Yes, I'm sure he is. Well . . . thanks for answering my questions! Have a good--

A: Wait, don't you want to hear what I'm going to wear to the Oscars? . . .

CONVERSATION TERMINATED

The next morning, Bridgette called Jill and told her about the interview.

"Maybe she really was having an affair with Tom Cruise," Jill said.

Bridgette snorted into the phone. "Yeah, right. The lady was a wacko, believe me."

"I used to pretend my Ken doll was real," Jill confided. "Sometimes, when I was sure my sister was asleep, I'd kiss him."

"Did he kiss back?"

Jill giggled.

"Hey, what are you eating?" Bridgette asked. She could hear Jill chewing.

"Maple syrup on a pretzel. It's the closest thing to

junk food we have." She paused. "Bridgette, do you really think there's such a thing as true love?"

"What do you mean?"

"I don't know," Jill said. "I just wonder sometimes if I'll ever find it, that's all."

Bridgette was beginning to wonder, too, especially when she thought about Aaron and his gagging faces, or Jacob, whose harsh laughter still rang in her ears. *But just because I haven't found that special someone yet, doesn't mean he isn't out there,* Bridgette reminded herself.

"True love exists," she said firmly.

As if on cue, the doorbell rang. Bridgette stretched the phone cord to look out the window.

There was a shiny red Volkswagen in the driveway, and her brother Trent was getting out of the driver's side. Then the passenger door opened, and the long, lean legs of his fiancée, Celia Davenport, appeared.

"Gotta go," Bridgette said. "Trent and Celia just drove up. They're staying until Tuesday."

"Are they in love?" Jill asked. "I mean really, truly in love?"

"Of course they are. They're getting married in less than a month, aren't they?"

"Call me later," Jill begged. "I want to hear every last detail."

Bridgette hung up the phone, then flew down the stairs two at a time. Mom and Dad were standing in the doorway with their backs to her. She squeezed between them and watched as Trent and Celia came up the walk.

Trent was wearing black jeans and a perfectly pressed denim shirt. His auburn hair bounced lightly against his collar. Celia was tall and thin, with long, silky blond hair. In her tight jeans and a bulky red sweater, she looked like someone straight out of the pages of *Vogue*.

An instant later, everyone was tangled up in a big hug. "Come in, come in," Mom gushed. "How was the drive? You must be tired. How about a cup of coffee?"

"Sounds good," Celia replied.

"When are they going to get a Starbucks around here?" Trent asked.

"Any day now," Dad said darkly. "The strip malls are spreading like a virus."

"Yes, but the real estate market is booming," Mom pointed out.

"Well, that's all that matters, isn't it?" Dad said sarcastically.

There was an uncomfortable pause as Mom muttered, "I'll make the coffee," and walked quickly into the kitchen.

"Come on in," Dad said, as if nothing had happened. "Brendan should be home from work soon." He strolled into the living room and sat in the blue easy chair.

Trent and Celia sat down on the sofa, thigh to thigh, holding hands. Bridgette sprawled out in front of the fireplace.

"After Philadelphia, I don't think I could ever live out here again," Trent announced. He glanced at Celia. "Listen, do you hear that?"

"Hear what?" she asked.

"Nothing."

They both laughed knowingly. Bridgette joined in. She felt the same way about boring old Newley.

"Here we go," her mother trilled, walking into the living room with a tray of coffee. She set it on the coffee table and said, "I'm so excited about the wedding, Celia. I haven't talked it over with Dermott yet, but I think we'll come on Thursday so I can meet with the caterers before the rehearsal dinner."

"I thought the wedding was on a Saturday," said Bridgette's dad.

"It is," Mom replied impatiently, "but the rehearsal dinner is Friday evening, and I need time to prepare."

"I can't close the store that long," Dad said, shaking his head. "Now that Suzie is gone—"

"So hire somebody else already!" Mom snapped,

slamming her coffee cup on the table. "The world keeps turning, you know."

The room fell silent as Mom and Dad glared at each other. *What is the matter with you two?* Bridgette felt like screaming.

"Let's go up and get unpacked," Celia suggested after an awkward silence.

Trent nodded, and they hurried up the stairs. Bridgette followed, eager to escape the tension that hung between her parents. The three of them walked into Trent's old bedroom and closed the door.

"That was embarrassing," Celia said.

"What's up, Bridge?" Trent asked.

She shrugged. "I don't know. It started at the end of the summer. They're constantly snapping at each other. Either that, or ignoring each other completely."

"Mid-life crisis," Celia said with a knowing nod. "My father had one. First he started talking about selling his business and opening a motorcycle shop. Then he bought a Harley and took off on a cross-country trip. He hit a tree somewhere out in Indiana, and my mother had to go and bring him home."

"That doesn't sound like something Dad would do," Bridgette said. "He loves the antique shop. Plus, he can't even balance on Brendan's scooter."

"If you ask me, it's Mom," Trent said. "The first kid's getting married, the next one's off to college next year, and you'll be starting high school. I took Psych 101. The stage is set for classic Empty Nest Syndrome."

Mid-life crisis. Empty Nest Syndrome. Wow, thought Bridgette, *Trent and Celia know about stuff I can't even begin to grasp.*

That gave her an idea. "I'm writing a paper for English class about love," she said. "Can I interview you guys about your relationship?"

"Sure," they replied at the exact same time. They exchanged a glance and burst out laughing. Trent slipped his arm around Celia's waist. She leaned her head against his shoulder.

Bridgette stared enviously. Love, red-hot as the coils in a toaster oven, was radiating between them.

Please, Cupid, Bridgette prayed, *bring me a love like that.*

Dear Cupid,

Thank you, thank you, a million times, thank you!

That's assuming that what just happened to me was your doing. Come to think of it, maybe your job description doesn't include finding secret admirers for love-starved eighth-grade girls. Maybe you only shoot your arrow once the two potential lovebirds are gazing into each other's eyes.

Or maybe this is a test. If I can figure out who my secret admirer is and meet him face-to-face, THEN you'll send your arrow flying.

I don't know. But I do know I feel like I'm dancing on the moon, soaring on a comet, swinging on Saturn's rings. In short, I'm in love!

It happened yesterday when school ended. I walked to my locker and found Vaughn leaning against it.

"This is a fifteen-minute parking zone," I said.

"Where's your meter maid uniform?" he asked.

"In an effort to boost morale, Mondays have been designated Casual Days," I replied. "This is my uniform."

He laughed. "Whatever you say, Zebra Lady. I just thought we could walk over to the pool together." He moved aside so I could open my locker.

As the door swung open, a folded piece of paper fell to the floor. I picked it up and opened it. Then I read the words that would change my life:

"I love your hair, your eyes, your freckles. I love the way you laugh and the sound of your voice. Maybe someday I'll have the courage to introduce myself. But how do you talk to a goddess? Love, Your Secret Admirer"

My heart seemed to stop as my eyes scanned the words. Then it kicked in again, only twice as fast and so loud I was sure Vaughn could hear the pounding.

"What's that?" he asked, pointing to the note.

"Oh, it's from Cassie," I lied and shoved it into my backpack.

Later, when swim practice ended, I took out the note and read it again. Cupid, do you remember that Love Links game I made up with Cassie and Jill, the one where we list everything we hope true love will be? Well, finding a love letter in my locker has always been at the top of my list. And now, it's actually come true!

I've read the note about a hundred times since I got home. It was typed on a computer, so unfortunately I can't identify the author by his handwriting. All I can do is wait and hope that someday soon my Secret Admirer will walk up and introduce himself to me. And when he does, Cupid, I hope your arrow will be ready.

TRANSCRIPT OF INTERVIEW #3

Subject: Trent Carley, male, age 24, unmarried, painter, fundraiser for an art museum

Q: How did you and Celia meet?
A: I brought in a slide of one of my paintings to show my boss. Celia walked by and saw it. She was really impressed with my work. One thing led to another and, well, here we are.

Q: In love.
A: Forever and always. Celia and I are more than best friends, more than lovers. We're soul mates.

Q: That's why you're getting married.
A: Right. And we're not rushing into it, the way Mom and Dad seem to think we are. Celia and I have been together for more than a year. We've talked a lot about our future, and we're in total agreement.

Q: About what?
A: Everything! Like having kids, for example. They're fine for some people, but not us. Our work is too important to us. Especially me. I plan on going places in the art world. I can't be tied down with kids like Mom and Dad are. Celia feels the same way.

Q: So you've both got the same goals. You want to be famous artists?

A: Of course! Well . . . it's a little bit different in Celia's case. I mean, she loves to throw pots, but she's happy just to do it for fun and let my success be the main focus. Anyway, pottery isn't exactly art, you know. It's more of a craft, like jewelry-making or glass-blowing.

Q: Do you and Celia ever fight?

A: (laughter) Everybody fights once in a while.

Q: What do you fight about?

A: Well, for instance, Celia can be a total slob sometimes. She leaves dirty plates in the sink, throws her clothes on the floor, forgets to empty the wastebaskets. It really irritates me. I've tried to explain to Celia that I can't focus on my painting with all her junk around. She understands. She's trying to improve.

Q: So you always work it out.

A: All it takes is one kiss, and we forget we were ever angry. Like they say in that movie LOVE STORY: "Love is never having to say you're sorry."

TRANSCRIPT OF INTERVIEW #4

Subject: Celia Davenport, female, age 25, unmarried, potter, slide librarian at an art museum

Q: How did you and Trent meet?
A: (laughter) It was so cute. Trent had brought in a slide of one of his paintings, and he was showing it around. To be honest, landscapes have never done much for me, and this one wasn't even particularly good. But what did impress me was Trent. He was so excited about his work, so animated. And gorgeous. Those eyes, those cheekbones, those ears. Hot!

Q: You think his ears are hot?
A: I think every inch of him is! But it's more than that. It's his personality, his spirit, his essence. We're soul mates.

Q: That's what Trent said, too.
A: I'm not surprised. We share everything. We're like two halves of a whole.

Q: Trent said you don't want to have children.
A: Well . . . not now, of course. But down the road, for sure. Trent's really focused on his career for the moment, and that's fine. But deep down, I know

he's looking forward to having a family someday just as much as I am.

Q: He wants to be a famous artist.
A: He's got an ego the size of Texas! (laughter) I mean, I love that he has goals, but sometimes they're not very realistic. Let's just say I'm glad I'll be able to support us with my pottery business.

Q: Do you ever fight?
A: Like cats and dogs! He gets all worked up about the littlest things sometimes. But he realizes it, and he's trying to improve. Anyway, our fights never last long, and we always make up before we say good night.

Dear Cupid,

I don't get it. Trent and Celia seem like the perfect couple. I mean, they've got so much in common. They're both artists, they both love city life, and they're both good-looking, smart, and stylish. Plus, they can't keep their hands off each other. So how come when I interviewed each of them, they sounded like they hardly even knew each other? Meanwhile, they claim to be soul mates!

Then again, what do I know? Maybe they ARE soul mates. Maybe love doesn't have anything to do with everyday stuff like jobs or money or doing the laundry. Maybe it's much deeper and more mysterious than we ordinary human beings can even begin to comprehend. Is that true, Cupid? Do you have to have wings and a quiver of arrows on your back to get it?

But if it's true—if love is an unsolvable mystery— then how will I know when I find it myself? And how in the world will I ever be able to figure out what's going on with Mom and Dad?

Maybe the answer lies with my Secret Admirer. After all, experience is the best teacher. Isn't that what people say? Well, then, what I've got to do is meet him. When our eyes finally lock and our fingers touch, then I'll understand what love is all about. And then maybe, just maybe, I'll know how to help Mom and Dad.

Which means I've got to find out who my Secret Admirer is—and fast, Cupid. I've already put Cassie and Jill on the case. They're both asking around, trying to find out if anyone saw a boy near my locker the afternoon the note appeared.

Cassie says he must be an eighth-grader. "Seventh-grade boys are too immature to write notes like that," she said, "and a sixth-grader wouldn't have the guts."

Jill thinks it has to be someone even older, maybe a high-school boy who spotted me at the pool and then sneaked into the middle school to drop the note in my locker.

Either one would be fine with me. I just want to meet him. I've been studying the faces of the boys I pass in school, at the pool, at the mall, trying to figure out if one of them is him. On my face I wear a permanent welcoming expression. "Talk to me, Secret Admirer," it says. "I won't shoot you down."

Apparently my expression is working a little too well, because this morning Vaughn asked me to the Halloween Dance. It was weird, actually, and kind of annoying because the dance is almost a month away. Why is he asking me now?

Or maybe a better question is, why is he asking me, PERIOD? I mean, I like Vaughn OK, but not like that. We don't have anything in common. He's into computers and fighting robots and whatever else techno-heads get excited about. I've never even seen him read a book other than a comic book. And I'm pretty sure he's never been to a Broadway musical or watched a romantic movie in his entire life.

Besides, if I go to the Halloween Dance with anyone, it will be my Secret Admirer.

Of course, there was one brief, fleeting moment when I wondered if maybe Vaughn was my Secret Admirer. But then I realized there was no way he could be. Vaughn is not shy and sensitive and romantic. He's funny and honest and real. If he liked me, he'd lay it on the line.

Which I guess he did when he asked me to the dance. Poor guy. I hope I didn't hurt his feelings when I told him no.

P.S. Exciting news, Cupid! There was another note in my locker this afternoon! My Secret Admirer instructed me to write back and leave my letter under the snare drum in the band room. "Just stick it between the wiggly metal wires," he wrote.

I figure that means he's got to be a drummer. Who else would know there are metal wires under snare drums? I sure didn't.

Tomorrow I plan to slip into the band room during rehearsal and check out the drummers. I can just picture it. I'll scan their faces, and suddenly I'll find myself looking at some handsome kid I've known all my life but never really noticed before. He'll smile, and in that one, life-altering instant, I'll just know.

"It's you," I'll whisper as he drops his drumsticks and walks into my arms. "My Secret Admirer."

Oh, Cupid, just thinking about it makes my legs feel as limp and rubbery as a couple of garden hoses. Please promise me you'll be there. After you shoot that arrow, I might need you to pick me up off the floor!

Chapter Eleven

Bridgette was certain that if she looked up the word *disaster* in the virtual dictionary, she'd find a video clip of her week. Everything was going wrong. Everything.

It started on Tuesday. English had just ended and she was supposed to be heading for P.E. Instead, she slipped into the band room, clutching the note she had written to her Secret Admirer.

A couple kids were already there, tuning up their instruments. "Hi, Bridgette," Melinda Wattenberg called between trills on her flute. "What are you doing here?"

"I'm, uh . . . I'm thinking of taking up percussion," Bridgette said, glancing toward the top riser with its row of snare and bass drums. No one was standing behind them yet, so before Melinda could ask any more questions, Bridgette walked up and crouched over the first snare, pretending to study it. When she was sure no one was looking, she reached underneath, felt for the wires, and slipped her note between them.

"What are you doing to my drum?" a voice asked.

She gasped and looked up into the puzzled face of Jake Farley. "Nothing," she blurted.

"I'm just, uh . . . nothing."

Is he my Secret Admirer? Bridgette wondered as she stumbled down the risers. She hoped not. Jake lived on a farm (memories of her embarrassing fall into the cow patty came flooding back), bit his fingernails until they were bloody, and spent every other day in the principal's office.

Bridgette paused at the clarinet section to talk to Allison Pollard. But what she was really doing was waiting for the rest of the drummers to show up. As they arrived, she studied their faces, hoping for that moment when she would gaze into the eyes of her Secret Admirer and Cupid's arrow would fly.

But it didn't happen. Other than Jake, there were only two more drummers, a sixth-grader and a seventh-grader. Both were shorter than Bridgette, one had a bad case of zits, and neither of them glanced in her direction. They were too busy playing noisy drum rolls and joking around.

Weighted down with disappointment, Bridgette couldn't make herself move fast enough to get to P.E. before the bell.

When she got there, Coach Ranck made her lead the class in one hundred jumping jacks, and her fellow students glared at her as if they'd like to gather up all the sweat that was pouring down their faces and drown her in it.

Meanwhile, Vaughn was ignoring her. In English class, he buried his head in his poetry book and didn't even comment on her totally black outfit. ("Solidarity with the panthers!" she had planned to say.)

Without Vaughn's goofball laugh and endless wisecracks, the walks to the pool after school were long and boring. Bridgette wished she could talk to him and explain about the dance. It wasn't that she wouldn't enjoy going with him, it was just . . . well, how could she put it? "I like you, Vaughn, but I'm waiting for someone better to come along."

No, she couldn't say that. So she didn't say anything at all.

But her miserable week was nothing compared to what happened on Saturday.

"Happy birthday!" Bridgette and Brendan shouted as Mom walked into the kitchen. Mom's bleary eyes focused, and she broke into a smile.

"Thanks, kids. Oh, French toast! My favorite!"

Dad appeared a minute later. Bridgette served the food, and they all sang "Happy Birthday." Her father was smiling, her mother was smiling. It was like old times, and Bridgette felt so grateful, she wanted to hug everyone.

"Oh, Bridgette, I love it!" Mom cried as she opened the gift certificate for a facial at Natural Wonders Spa and Salon. "I want you to come with me. In fact, let's see if they can take us this morning."

"I thought Bridgette had to clean her room this morning," Brendan grumbled. "You said *I* had to."

"You can both do it tomorrow," Mom replied, dialing the spa.

"May I get you a drink?" a youthful male voice asked. "Water? Soda? Coffee?"

Bridgette and her mother were sprawled out on massage tables with green clay on their faces and lemon slices over their eyes.

"Water would be lovely," Mom murmured contentedly. Bridgette lifted one lemon slice and found herself blinking into the gray-green eyes of the towel boy—a good-looking teenager.

"Uh, yes, um . . ." she muttered, racking her brain for something clever and fascinating to say. Finally, she gave up and said, "Coke, please."

As the boy walked away, Mom's cell phone began to ring. "Oh, darn," she said, groping in her bag. "It's probably a client. I'd better take it." She found the phone and held it a couple of inches from her ear. "Josephine Carley speaking," she said. "What? I can't hear you. Speak up."

Suddenly Mom's expression hardened, causing the clay around her eyes to crack. "Now? But we're right in the middle of our facial. Besides, this is my birthday."

"What's going on?" Bridgette whispered, squinting around the lemon slices. "Who is it?"

Mom ignored her. "You can't just whisk her away like that . . . (pause) . . . Well, call back and see if you can go another day." Mom pressed END and flung the phone into her bag.

"What was all that about?" Bridgette asked.

"Somehow your father got his hands on two tickets to the matinee performance of *Phantom of the Opera* in Harrisburg. He wanted to pick you up and drive there right now."

"*Phantom of the Opera!*" Bridgette cried. "Mom, it's the national touring company. They're only in town for two weeks."

Mom groaned. "I know, honey, but today? Now? I thought we were going to spend the day together. I was looking forward to—"

Suddenly, the door to the salon flew open and in walked Dad.

"Bridgette," he exclaimed, "did your mother tell you I snagged *Phantom* tickets?"

Bridgette didn't know what to say. She didn't want to disappoint her mother, especially on her birthday, and it *was* kind of thoughtless of Dad to just barge in on them like this.

But every fiber of Bridgette's being was longing to throw her arms around her father and cry, "Thank you, thank you, thank you!"

Mom sat up. The lemon slices fell from her eyes. "This isn't fair," she said angrily. "You're making her choose between us."

The spa owner hurried over. "Lie down, Mrs. Carley," she fussed. "To remove worry lines, you must keep the lemons in place for a full thirty minutes."

Ignoring the woman, Dad glared at Mom. "This isn't about you. It's about Bridgette. Can't you see how special this is to her? Anyway, what's the big deal? We'll celebrate your birthday tomorrow."

The spa owner reappeared with new lemon slices, but Mom waved her away. "I don't want to celebrate tomorrow," she snapped. "My birthday is today."

Dad took Bridgette's hand. He looked relaxed, but his fingernails were digging into her palm. "We have to leave now or we won't make the show," he said. "We'll be back by seven, Josie. Then we'll all go out to dinner."

"Take your hands off her," Mom ordered.

People were turning to look at them. "Mom, Dad," Bridgette whispered, "please."

"Come on, sweetie." Dad pulled her up off the table. "Wipe your face off, and let's go."

Bridgette hesitated. Out of the corner of her eye, she noticed her mother dipping her hand into the jar of green clay beside the massage table.

"Mom, no—!" she cried. But it was too late. Mom scooped up a glob of clay and threw it at Dad. It hit his cheek and fell to the floor with a plop.

The spa owner gasped. The other clients stared. Bridgette could feel her cheeks growing hot and red.

Dad just laughed and shook his head. "How very mature of you, Josie." Then he grabbed Bridgette's arm and led her toward the door.

"Dermott," Mom warned, "don't you dare . . ." She jumped to her feet and strode toward them.

Halfway there, she slipped on a blob of wet clay, skidded, and slammed to the floor.

"My ankle!" Bridgette's mother wailed. "I think I broke my ankle!"

As Bridgette ran to her mother's side, she noticed the towel boy standing by the counter with a tray of drinks in his hands. He seemed to be smiling at Bridgette. *Hey, maybe this is what they mean by "meeting 'cute,'"* she thought hopefully.

Then she looked more closely. The towel boy was smiling, all right—in fact, he was laughing, and the look in his eyes said it all. He thought Bridgette and her parents were embarrassing, pathetic, and hopelessly dysfunctional.

Bridgette felt like crying. *He's right,* she told herself.

Dear Cupid,

Mom's ankle isn't broken, just badly sprained. Of course, we didn't find that out until the ambulance took her to the hospital and we waited about three hours in the emergency room. By then it was too late to make it to PHANTOM, so we just hung around the house. Mom slept, Dad puttered in the garage, and Brendan and I popped DOCTOR ZHIVAGO into the VCR.

As Omar Sharif trudged through a blizzard in war-torn Russia searching for Julie Christie, I asked Brendan if he thought Mom and Dad were going to get divorced.

"I don't know," Brendan muttered. "But look at this camera angle, the way the icicles frame his face. It's brilliant." There's no point in talking to Brendan, Cupid. When things get rough, he just goes to the movies.

I tried to follow his example and lose myself in Omar's haunted, lovelorn eyes. But I couldn't stop thinking about Mom and Dad. Once upon a time, they were madly in love. But now look at them. They can barely be in the same room with each other without causing a public disturbance.

Cupid, I'm scared. What if Mom and Dad really do

break up? Brendan is going off to college next year, but what about me? Where would I live? Would I have to shuttle back and forth between two houses? Would I have to take sides?

And what about my own love life? I mean, if my parents could make such a huge relationship mistake, maybe I will, too. I'll find Mr. Right, only to discover he's Mr. Oh-So-Wrong in disguise.

No, no, no. I'm never going to end up like my mom and dad—arguing and criticizing and flinging things at each other like preschoolers. When I meet my Secret Admirer, it's going to be completely different. No shouting. No complaining. No sarcastic comments. Just everlasting love, hot enough to melt a Russian blizzard.

By the way, letter number three came today, Cupid! Here's what it said: "Dearest Bridgette, you are beautiful, smart, and funny. What if I'm not good enough for you? What if you laugh in my face? I dream of us being together, but I'm scared. Please write back and tell me I'm not wasting my time. Love, Your Secret Admirer"

After I read the letter, I took a long, hard look at Jake Farley. Except for those chewed-up fingers, and his ears—which have droopy lobes and kind of stick out—he's not bad looking. Maybe what's happening is one of those Cinderella scenarios, like in the movie SHE'S ALL THAT. Maybe beneath Jake's unappealing exterior lies a sensitive, caring guy who's madly in love with me but is just too shy to say it. And maybe with a little TLC, I could transform him into a total heartthrob.

Crazy? No crazier than the rest of my life. But I don't think I can risk approaching Jake. I mean, what if he's the wrong guy? Better to just write back and leave the approaching up to my Secret Admirer, whoever he may be.

Gotta go, Cupid. I've got a love letter to write.

Subject: male, age 72, widowed, retired

Q: Are you in a relationship?
A: You mean, am I married? Well, I was, for fifty-two beautiful years. My wife passed away last year.

Q: Oh. I'm sorry.
A: Me, too. There isn't a day that goes by that I don't miss her.

Q: How did you meet?
A: At a dance. I was home from the war-- the Big One, that is, World War II--and working in a gas station. No direction, didn't know what I wanted to do with my life. Clara changed all that. I wanted to make something of myself so she'd take me seriously. So I went to night school and got a job with Esso. It's called Exxon now.

Q: And then you asked her to marry you?
A: Yep, but she said no. I think she was playing hard to get. I didn't give up, though. I romanced her. Brought her flowers and candy. I even sang to her outside her window.

Q: Sounds romantic!
A: (laughs) We were crazy back then, so in love we couldn't think straight. But, you know, it gets exhausting feeling

like that all the time. You can't eat, can't sleep. Personally, it gave me the runs! I was happy when she finally said yes so we could settle down and start a family.

Q: Did having kids change things?
A: Oh, sure. Always does. The kids became the center of our lives, and all that hot and heavy stuff went out the window.

Q: How did the two of you handle that?
A: Not well. We grew apart. Finally, when our last kid went off to college, we realized we'd become strangers to each other.

Q: What did you do?
A: We thought about getting a divorce. Then we decided to give the marriage another try.

Q: And you fell in love with each other all over again?
A: Yes, but maybe not the way you're thinking. There were no flowers or candy this time. No love songs outside the window. Things were quieter, calmer, and a lot more real.

Q: What do you mean?
A: We just learned to appreciate each other more and not take each other for

granted. I realized I loved my wife, not for her looks or her sex appeal or any of that foolishness, but for the way she was always there, day after day, taking care of things. Taking care of me.

Q: But what about romance?
A: Oh, there was some of that, too. But as you get older, well, it becomes less important. What you want is companionship, understanding. Clara gave me all that. I tried to give as good as I got, too, especially toward the end, when she was sick and in pain.

Q: You were there for her.
A: For better or worse, for richer or poorer, in sickness and in health, till death do us part. You don't need a sociological survey to figure that out. All you have to do is live as long as I have.

Chapter Twelve

"What's that?" Brendan asked, glancing up from his book, *Star Wars: A Scene-by-Scene Analysis.*

He and Bridgette were riding with their parents in the car, on their way to Philadelphia for Trent and Celia's wedding.

"Nothing," Bridgette muttered, shoving the latest letter from her Secret Admirer into her jeans' pocket and trying not to blush. She turned toward the window and pretended to be interested in the passing scenery—the same yawn-producing cows and cornfields she'd known all her life.

Mom looked over the front seat. "What are you reading, Bridgette?" she asked, spotting the book that was sticking out of Bridgette's backpack.

Uh-oh. Mom didn't even like her reading romance novels. What would she think of *The Book of Love: A History of Mating and Marriage?* "It's for my research paper," Bridgette said, handing over the book. "I'm writing about courtship in the Middle Ages."

It was a lie, of course, but bringing up her real topic didn't seem like a good idea, what with Mom and Dad barely speaking to each other and an hour-long road trip ahead of them.

"Slow down, Dermott!" Mom cried suddenly. "You're much too close to that truck."

"Relax," Dad said. "Everything's under control."

"That's what you said a few minutes ago when you almost sideswiped that trailer."

"Look, do *you* want to drive?" Dad snapped. "If not, mind your own business."

Bridgette laughed uncomfortably. "Now, come on, you two."

"You're right," Mom said, sighing. "This is supposed to be a happy family weekend." She handed the book back to Bridgette, then folded her arms and stared out the window with a tight smile on her face.

No one said another word for the next hour. In the back seat, Bridgette leaned against the door and thought about her last telephone interview. The old man she'd spoken with had said he didn't learn to appreciate his wife until they almost broke up.

Is that what's going to happen with Mom and Dad? she wondered. Would their marriage have to break apart before it could be put back together again?

But what if it collapsed and her parents couldn't— or wouldn't—repair things?

Bridgette pushed that scary thought from her mind by reaching into her pocket and touching the letter from her Secret Admirer. Closing her eyes, she pictured herself sailing away from the suffocating silence of the car, over the cows and cornfields, and into the arms of her mystery man.

"Oh, my, everything looks lovely!" exclaimed Mrs. Torelli, Celia's mother. "Just exquisite!"

The wedding rehearsal was over, and the guests were filing into the Pennsbury Inn for the rehearsal dinner. Trent and Celia's friends swarmed through the door, laughing and joking as they headed for the hors d'oeuvres. The best man produced a Nerf football from his coat pocket and tossed it to Trent. Celia and her bridesmaids rolled their eyes.

"Thank you, Deb," Bridgette's mother said. Mom was officially off crutches now, but she still had a limp from her fall on the wet clay. "Now let me show you where you're sitting."

Mrs. Torelli scanned the place cards at each table setting. Suddenly, she frowned. "Josie, I'm only five seats away from Celia's father."

"Yes, um, that's true. But he's on the other side of the table and—"

"No. I can't sit near my ex-husband. You'll have to move me."

Mom shot Bridgette a "give me a break" look. The long banquet table was filling up with guests. A few people had already started drinking from their water glasses.

"Maybe you can find someone to change places with you," Mom suggested. "Possibly down at the other end of the table?"

"But I want to be near Celia."

Mom took a long, slow breath. "I'll see what I can do," she said.

Bridgette edged away from the adults, eager to lose herself among Trent and Celia's friends. She noticed Brendan shooting a video of the ushers, who belted out a joking, off-key rendition of "Wild Thing." Two of the bridesmaids stood on chairs doing a go-go dance, while the rest of the bridal party laughed and clapped. Other guests milled around the bar, where video clips of Trent and Celia as small children were being projected onto the wall.

But where were the stars of the video? Bridgette scanned the room. Finally she spotted them disappearing down the hallway that led to the pay phones.

I bet they're off to steal a secret kiss, Bridgette thought with a sigh. *How romantic!* She followed quietly behind.

But as she got closer, she heard Celia's voice cut through the murmur of the crowd. "How could you say a thing like that?" she demanded. "It's as if you think my pottery is just a hobby or something."

Bridgette froze, her heart thumping. She knew she should walk away, but her feet seemed to be sinking into the carpet.

"I never said that, Celia." It was Trent's voice, and he sounded indignant. "You're putting words in my mouth."

"Then what *did* you say?" Celia asked.

"Nothing really. I just don't think you're as committed to your work as I am to mine. I mean, in order to succeed in today's art world, you have to have a unique vision, and—"

"You don't think my work is *unique?*"

"It's beautiful. But let's face it, Celia, these are pots we're talking about. How unique can they—"

A clinking sound drowned out Trent's words. Bridgette turned to see her mother briskly tapping a water glass with a spoon. "Would everyone please be seated?" she called. "We're about to start dinner."

Trent and Celia darted past Bridgette and hurried to their seats without looking at each other. Soon a parade of waiters marched out of the kitchen, carrying plates of food. Bridgette, sitting beside her mother, tried to concentrate on the conversations of the people around her. But she couldn't stop thinking about Trent and Celia. Their wedding was less than twenty-four hours away. Why were they arguing?

Bridgette's mom stood up, clinking her glass with her spoon again.

"Welcome, everyone," she said brightly. "As the parents of the groom, Dermott and I would like to say how pleased we are to see you all here, and to have a chance to meet some of Trent and Celia's friends. And, of course, it's been a delight getting to know Celia's parents, Deb Torelli and Bob Davenport."

Before Bridgette's mother could say another word, Mr. Davenport jumped up and raised his glass. He looked a little unsteady on his feet as he blurted, "I wanna propose a toast. But first, I wanna say I'm glad the wedding is tomorrow, because I can't take any more planning."

Everybody laughed. Bridgette's father called, "Hear, hear!"

The only person not laughing was Celia's mother. "Sit down, Bob," she hissed from her new seat near the end of the table.

Mr. Davenport ignored her. "If I hafta hear one more discussion about what the bridesmaids should wear," he slurred, "or where we're orderin' the cake, I'll go out of my ever-lovin' mind. And the cat fights! Ya put the mothers of the bride and groom in the same room together, and believe me, sparks are gonna fly!"

Mom turned red with embarrassment. Celia's mother leaped to her feet and tried to cut in. "I'd like to propose a toast to Trent and—"

"Sit down, Deb, I'm not finished yet," said Mr. Davenport.

"Yes, you are." She glanced over the crowd. "I want to apologize for—"

"For being a pain in the neck!" Mr. Davenport broke in. The room fell silent except for a few nervous titters. Everyone stared at Celia's parents, waiting to see what would happen next. Everyone, that is, except Trent and Celia, who were whispering heatedly to each other. One look at their pinched faces, and Bridgette knew they were arguing again.

Suddenly, Celia pushed back her chair and cried, "Trent, how could you?"

The guests' heads snapped toward them like spectators at the final match of Wimbledon.

"Celia," Trent stammered, "I—I didn't mean . . . I just . . ."

Celia sprung from her chair and bolted out of the room.

Chapter Thirteen

For one long moment, it seemed to Bridgette as if someone had pressed the pause button on the VCR of life. Everyone was frozen, staring at Celia's empty chair. Then Trent jumped up and ran after her, and instantly everything switched to fast forward.

Trent and Celia's friends began talking and shouting and ordering each other around. "Go after them!" someone cried.

"They have to work this out themselves," another voice said.

"What? You expect me to stay here and watch their relationship fall apart?" the maid of honor exclaimed. She dashed out of the room, followed by the ushers and the bridesmaids.

Celia's mother was crying and wringing her hands. Mr. Davenport tossed back another drink.

"Dermott, do something," Mom ordered.

"What do you expect me to do?" he asked.

"Oh, forget it. You're no help at all," she grumbled. She headed for the door. Bridgette ran after her.

"Pre-wedding jitters," Mom said to the bewildered coat-check girl as they hurried out of the restaurant. "Happens all the time. A couple of smooches and it will all be over."

As they reached the parking lot, a red Volkswagen screeched past them and roared into the street. Bridgette saw a strand of silky blond hair streaming out the window.

A moment later, Trent appeared out of the darkness. "I don't know what happened."

Bridgette thought about mentioning their argument in the hallway, but then she'd have to admit that she had been eavesdropping.

Just then, Bridgette's dad came out of the restaurant, followed by Celia's parents. "Did you find her?" he asked Trent.

"Yeah," Trent answered. "But she's gone now. She almost ran me over."

The maid of honor joined them. "She's got a key to my place. Maybe she went there."

"Or to her apartment," Celia's mother suggested.

"Let's split up," Mom said. She rummaged in her purse for a pen. "We'll exchange cell phone numbers and call if we find her."

Bridgette looked out the window as Dad steered the car through the crowded streets of downtown Philadelphia. Beside her, Brendan stared down at his *Star Wars* book.

"Dozens of invitations sent," Mom grumbled, "the hall rented, the honeymoon booked. I cannot believe this is happening."

"Better now than later," Dad said. "Marriage is a big commitment. If you make a mistake, you're basically stuck."

Mom cast a sideways glance at him. But before she could say anything, her cell phone rang.

"Hello?" she said. "What? Oh, glory hallelujah! We're on our way." She tossed down the phone. "The bridesmaids found Celia. She's in some all-night diner over in Camden."

Dad followed Mom's directions, and a few minutes later they were pulling into the parking lot of a shiny, silver-sided diner with a blue neon OPEN ALL NIGHT sign in the window.

They hurried inside and found Celia in a back booth, surrounded by her bridesmaids. Her mascara was smudged, and her cheeks were tear stained.

". . . and then he told me he hates children," she sniffed. "Hates them. And just last week he said my niece was adorable."

Celia's friends clucked sympathetically. Someone handed her a Kleenex, and she blew her nose. Then she looked up and cried, "Go away! I have nothing to say to you."

Bridgette and her startled family stopped in their tracks. But then Bridgette realized Celia wasn't looking at them. She was looking at Trent and his best man, who had just walked in the door. Celia's parents were right behind him.

To Bridgette's surprise, her brother strode straight toward *her*, not Celia, and asked, "When you interviewed Celia, did she tell you she wanted to have children?"

Uh-oh. Bridgette felt like a cornered rabbit. Should she tell the truth? How would Trent react if she did? What about Celia? "Well . . . uh . . ." Bridgette stammered.

"I said I wanted them *someday*," Celia broke in. "I thought you would, too, once you'd had a couple of years to see if your painting career panned out."

"Well, gee, that's a real vote of confidence," Trent said. "Believe it or not, Celia, I *am* going to succeed. Because, unlike you, I consider art the most important thing in my life. More important than money, more important than kids, more important than—"

"Go on and say it. More important than me."

Trent shook his head in disgust. "You know, when Bridgette asked me if we ever fight, I told her it was no big deal. But the truth is, you're constantly picking fights with me."

"Me? I leave a few dishes in the sink, and you lay into me as if I'd slashed your canvas."

"Leaving a half-empty coffee cup sitting right on my easel, Celia, is pretty passive-aggressive, don't you think?"

"You told Bridgette I'm passive-aggressive?"

"No," Trent said, "I told her you're a slob!"

"Wait a minute," Mrs. Torelli interrupted. "Why do you keep talking about Bridgette? What does she have to do with all this?"

Bridgette swallowed hard as all eyes turned toward her. The bright fluorescent lights felt like spotlights aimed at her guilty face. "I interviewed Trent and Celia for my school report," she explained.

"I thought your paper was about courtship in the Middle Ages," Dad said.

"Actually," Bridgette admitted, "it's more about the twenty-first century."

"When I found out some of the things Celia told Bridgette," Trent explained, "I was really shocked. It turns out Celia doesn't understand me at all."

"Look who's talking," Celia said. "I should thank Bridgette, really. If she hadn't asked all those probing questions, I never would have realized what a terrible mistake I was making."

"Now, now," Celia's mother said soothingly. "I'm sure this is all just a misunderstanding. If Bridgette hadn't gotten between you two lovebirds and started trouble—"

"What are you implying?" Mom asked. "That this is my daughter's fault?"

"Mom," Bridgette whispered, "please."

"Look, she's a teenager," Celia's mother replied. "You have to keep a tight rein on them at that age."

"I wish someone would keep a tight rein on *you*, Deb," Mr. Davenport said, hee-hawing loudly.

Mom ignored him and exclaimed, "Bridgette isn't the one who walked out of the rehearsal dinner!"

"Josephine, calm down," Dad broke in.

"Calm down? This woman's trying to blame our daughter for breaking up Trent and Celia. Just because she asked the two of them a few innocent questions . . ."

"How do you know what Bridgette asked?" Dad demanded. "You weren't there. The truth is, you have no idea what's going on with Bridgette or Trent or anyone else in this family. All you care about is *your* job, *your* needs, *your*—"

Bridgette's throat was burning. She could feel hot tears welling up in the corners of her eyes. "Daddy, don't," she pleaded.

"You tell 'em, buddy," Mr. Davenport said, thumping Dad's shoulder.

"Shut up, Bob," Celia's mother ordered.

"I think you should all shut up!" Bridgette shouted. "I mean, what's wrong with you people? You yell and complain and blame each other for everything. Don't you realize weddings are supposed to be about togetherness and promises and happily-ever-after? They're supposed to be about true love!"

The diner was silent. Everyone—Trent, Celia, the bridesmaids, even the other customers and the waitresses—were staring at Bridgette.

Her dad was the first to speak. "I wish it were that simple, Bridgette." He took a deep breath and let the air out through his lips. "The truth is, marriage is a rocky road. It's best Trent and Celia learn that now before they take such a big step. I certainly wish I had." Then he turned and walked away.

"Dermott!" Mom called. "Where are you going?"

But Dad was already out the door. Mom limped after him. Bridgette followed, too upset to care whether people were whispering about her, too upset even to wipe away the tears that were streaming down her face.

Out in the parking lot, Dad got into the car and started the engine. Mom lunged for the door handle, but before she could grab it, he threw the car into reverse and shot backward.

As Bridgette watched with dismay, her father peeled out of the parking lot and disappeared into the night.

Dear Cupid,

All I wanted to do was find out what true love means. That, and maybe understand why my previously loving parents have become arch enemies. Instead, two marriages have self-destructed, and it's all my fault.

Cassie and Jill say it would have happened anyway, but I'm not so sure. If I hadn't interviewed Trent and Celia for my research paper, would they have called off the wedding? I don't think so. That night at the diner, they both looked so hurt and miserable, I felt like the anti-Cupid.

Cassie still insists it was for the best. "They really did have some major issues," she pointed out.

Maybe so. But why did I have to be the one to bring them all to the surface?

And anyway, nothing compares to how rotten I felt when Dad floored the car out of the diner parking lot. That was all my fault, too. If it weren't for my big speech about true love and happily-ever-after, Dad wouldn't have felt the need to point out how his marriage is NOT like that. And he never would have walked out.

When Trent drove us back to our motel, we found a phone message from Dad saying he'd taken the train back to Newley. Mom, Brendan, and I drove back the next day. By the time we got back, Dad had checked into a motel in Lancaster. Now Mom and Dad haven't spoken—or even laid eyes on each other—for almost two weeks.

Cupid, I keep remembering that story Cassie told me about her Aunt Rita and Uncle Joe, the ones who got into a huge fight in front of the entire family on Christmas Eve.

Sounds a lot like Mom and Dad. They never used to get into fights in public places. They never fought, period. So what's next? Cassie said her aunt and uncle were separated by New Year's Day. It looks like that's what's going to happen to my parents.

Last night, way past midnight, I woke up and heard a strange whimpering sound outside my door. I got up and tiptoed into the hall. The bathroom door was open a crack and the light was on. As I crept closer, I saw Mom standing at the sink with a bottle of Dad's aftershave in her hand. Her hair was a mess and her face was streaked with tears.

My chest felt so tight, I couldn't inhale. In our family, my dad is the weepy one. He cries at senti-mental movies, McDonald's commercials, even parades. Mom never sheds a tear. But now she was flat-out sobbing.

I wondered if should I go in and try to comfort her. Apologize for screwing up Trent and Celia's wedding? Beg her to explain why she and my father no longer loved each other?

Before I could decide, she flung the aftershave bottle at the wall. I heard the sound of shattering glass, and a second later my nostrils were filled with the scent of peppermint and cloves. It reminded me of Dad, and suddenly I felt so sad, so scared, so sick to my stomach that all I could do was stumble back to bed and hide under the covers. I stayed there, huddled in a tight little ball, until morning.

Dear Cupid,

Something incredible has happened!

After last night, I thought I'd never smile again. Then I went to school and opened my locker. A small, folded piece of paper fell to the floor—a note from my Secret Admirer. My heart leaped. For the first time since I came home from Philadelphia, I felt that maybe there was a reason to go on breathing.

I opened the paper and here's what it said:

"Bridgette, my beloved, I can't hold back any longer. Meet me under the big oak tree behind the middle school at seven o'clock tonight. All my love, Your Secret Admirer."

Is it too good to be true? No, I can't believe that. Maybe Mom and Dad and Trent and Celia haven't found true love, but that doesn't mean it doesn't exist. It's out there, I just know it, and in a few short hours, I'm going to find it.

My Secret Admirer awaits—tonight!

Chapter Fourteen

Bridgette coasted into the middle-school parking lot and let out a grateful sigh. She'd never ridden her bike in the dark before, and she prayed she'd never have to do it again.

She closed her eyes and took a deep breath. *My parents would freak if they knew I was here,* she thought.

But they didn't know. Dad was still living at the motel, and Mom was working late. Only Brendan was home, and he was too busy scarfing pizza and watching *The Godfather, Part III* to notice she was gone.

Bridgette took another deep breath and shivered in the cold night air. She parked her bike in the bike rack, then hugged her chest and slipped her hands under her armpits. Carefully, she made her way around to the side of the school. It was dark, but a faint glow from the playing fields out back lit the way for her.

As she edged forward, she tried to picture the boy she was about to meet. Was it Jake Farley? Another boy from her class?

Maybe, as Jill had suggested, it was someone from the high school. Bridgette could almost see his tall, muscular body, his high cheekbones, his dark, sensitive eyes gazing at her adoringly.

At last, she turned the corner and saw the oak tree. Illuminated by a bright light on the roof of the school, the tree looked dramatic and mysterious. Instantly, Bridgette's heart began pounding like surf against the shore. Was her Secret Admirer waiting in the shadows beneath the tree? Maybe he was watching her right now.

My hair! she thought with horror. She scooted back around the corner and ran her hands through her curls. Then she straightened her shoulders and rounded the corner for a second time.

Bridgette walked to the tree on legs so wobbly she almost tripped on a sprinkler nozzle that was buried in the grass. *OK,* she told herself, *relax. Remember, he's just as nervous as you are.*

A sudden scraping sound—it seemed to come from somewhere up in the tree—made Bridgette jump. Was it an animal? She stepped back, looked up into the branches, and—

SPLOOSH!

Icy water hit her face. She shrieked and stumbled backward as the water poured over her shoulders and across her chest. It dripped down the collar of her shirt, raising goosebumps on the back of her neck.

"Wha—wha—" she gulped.

Suddenly, a dark figure dropped from the tree and landed in front of her with a thud. Bridgette shrieked again and fell back into the grass.

"That was for ratting on me to Tindall," a voice growled.

Bridgette blinked her eyes and tried to focus through a blur of freezing water and stunned tears. There, standing in front of her, was Aaron Shoening. He had his hands on his hips and a satisfied smirk on his face.

"You—*you're* my Secret Admirer?" she sputtered, hoping with all her heart and soul she was wrong.

He laughed. "That's me, babe. And let me give you a word of advice. If you ever want to find a real boyfriend, you're going to have to stop being such a snotty, tattletale, pain-in-the-butt."

Aaron reached up into the tree and shook the branches. An empty plastic bucket with a rope tied to the handle fell to the ground.

"It wasn't easy getting that bucket of water up in the tree," he remarked. He turned and looked at Bridgette, huddled and shivering in the grass. "But it was worth it."

Then he picked up the bucket and strolled off into the night.

Chapter Fifteen

"**S**o what happened?" Jill asked. "Did you meet him? Who is he?"

The questions came so fast, they sounded like one long sentence. "I don't really want to talk about it," Bridgette said into the telephone.

"Why not? Oh, Bridge, don't tell me the guy stood you up!"

"No, not exactly." Bridgette bit her lower lip and willed herself not to cry. "Look, I'll tell you about it tomorrow, OK?"

"Well . . . OK. If you're sure."

Bridgette could hear the disappointment in Jill's voice. *She probably thinks I want to tell Cassie first,* she thought.

But, of course, that wasn't true. Bridgette didn't want to tell *anyone* what had happened, not even her best friends. It was just too humiliating.

Unfortunately, there was one person who would want to tell the whole world. Aaron. He was probably calling everybody he knew right now, spreading the word. By tomorrow, the entire school would be laughing at Bridgette. She'd never live it down.

Bridgette hung up the phone and flopped back onto her bed. It had been almost an hour since she'd pedaled home from school, and she still felt like crying. *And to think I'd actually believed that turning in Aaron for cheating would make him fall in love with me.* She shook her head.

It was ridiculous. In fact, the whole idea of studying movie plots to learn about love was just plain absurd. She could see that now.

Bridgette closed her eyes and listened to the murmur of the TV drifting up from the den. She felt like marching downstairs and telling Brendan exactly what she thought of him and his moronic movies. But then she thought, *It's not Brendan's fault. It's mine for following the advice of a total geek who doesn't even have a girlfriend.*

She rolled onto her stomach and gazed at her desk, cluttered with books on love and marriage, printouts of Web pages dealing with romance, and transcripts of her phone interviews. She sighed. Trent and Celia were history. Mom and Dad were on the verge of divorce. And the people she'd interviewed on the phone seemed to think romance meant changing diapers and paying bills and giving each other an occasional peck on the cheek.

Bridgette felt like taking the whole pile of books and papers and burning it. But that wasn't an option. Her research paper was due in two weeks. She had to turn in something.

But what could she possibly write about? She didn't know a thing about true love. In fact, after all she'd been through, she wasn't even sure it existed. Maybe it was just something made up by corporate America to sell books and movies and greeting cards.

That was a depressing thought. If true love didn't exist, then there was no reason to expect her parents to make up, no reason to hope that Trent and Celia would go through with their marriage, no reason to keep searching for the boy of her dreams. He wasn't out there, and that was that.

Bridgette stood up and looked in the mirror. "OK, girl, you're off the hook," she said to her reflection. "You don't have to figure out what went wrong with Mom and Dad, or blame yourself for Trent and Celia's fight. And as for Aaron, he's a creep and he always will be."

Bridgette studied herself in the mirror. The hopeful, starry-eyed dreamer she used to be was gone. Instead, the girl who gazed back at her looked damp and bedraggled, lost and bewildered, like a puppy who'd been left out in the rain.

Disgusted, Bridgette turned away and sat down at her desk. She was just feeling sorry for herself, she decided. What she needed was to get busy, to lose herself in some interesting activity.

There was still that research report to write. Her eyes scanned the piles of books and papers on her desk. Then she noticed the tape recorder. She could always interview some more people about their romantic experiences.

Now, though, her expectations would be completely different. No longer would she be searching for someone whose love life matched her ridiculous fantasies. She was ready to face the hard truth about male-female relationships. Broken dreams? Lost love? Shattered hearts? "Bring 'em on," she muttered as she plugged in the tape recorder and connected the voice changer.

She picked up the phone and punched in some numbers. 5 . . . 6 . . . 2 . . . 3 . . . 1 . . . 4 . . .

With a gasp, Bridgette slammed down the receiver. The number she was dialing was her mother's office!

What was I doing? she asked herself.

Not that her mother was necessarily still at work. It was almost eight-fifteen. Most likely, she was on her way home. But what if she had actually answered the phone? *What a disaster!* Bridgette thought with a shudder.

Or would it have been? Suddenly an idea began to form in her head. She pulled her knees to her chest and sucked thoughtfully on the inside of her cheek.

With the voice changer hooked up, there was no way Mom could recognize Bridgette's voice. *I could interview her just the way I interviewed all the others,* Bridgette realized. Her mind began to reel, imagining the possibilities.

And then another thought struck her. If she could get Mom talking, why not Dad, too?

Can I really pull this off? She frowned and twisted a strand of damp hair around her finger. The thought of calling her parents and pretending to be an adult interviewer made her stomach churn. But she had to try. How many hours had she spent puzzling over her parents' disintegrating relationship? Maybe now she'd finally get some answers.

Bridgette pressed her hands to her chest, trying to slow down her galloping heart. "You can do this," she whispered. "You can do this."

Then she picked up the receiver and dialed.

TRANSCRIPT OF INTERVIEW #6

Subject: female, age 48, married, real-estate agent

Q: Good evening. This is the Carley . . . I mean, the Corelli Institute for Sociological Research. Do you have a minute to answer a few questions?
A: I'm on my way out the door. Questions about what?

Q: Male-female relationships.
A: You've picked the wrong person. I don't know a thing about male-female relationships, except that they stink.

Q: If you agree to a short interview, we'll send you a book of useful coupons.
A: Coupons for what?

Q: I've got one here for, uh . . . for a free facial at Natural Wonders Spa and Salon. And a massage, too.
A: (pause) You know, this is a funny coincidence. My son and his fiancée were just interviewed about the same subject. They broke up after they heard what each one said about the other. What did you say your organization was called again?

Q: The Corelli Institute for Sociological Research. We're doing a study for the federal government. I can assure you

that this interview is completely confidential.

A: (pause) Well, OK, go ahead. But make it quick. I've got to get home.

Q: **Are you currently in a relationship?**
A: To tell you the truth, I'm not sure. My husband moved out last week.

Q: **How long have you two been married?**
A: Almost twenty-five years. Gosh, I can't believe it's been that long. It's hard to imagine, but we were once crazy about each other.

Q: **What first attracted you to him?**
A: He was smart. Funny. Handsome. And there were so many things he was passionate about. He loved art history and architecture and antiques.

Q: **And you liked that?**
A: I did. But that was before kids and mortgages and college tuition. The things he loves don't make you rich.

Q: **Does he have a job?**
A: Oh, sure. He owns his own business. It did well for years, but lately the market's been changing. He doesn't know how to change with the times. Now his business is about to go under.

Q: **You mean bankrupt?**
A: It's a strong possibility. I offered

to help him fix the place up, make it
more contemporary, but forget it. He
doesn't want any help from me. He thinks
he knows it all.

Q: And that's why he moved out?
A: That's part of it. But the real
reason is, he's in love with someone
else.

Q: He is? I—I mean, how do you know?
A: I caught him in the arms of the woman
he works with. Or should I say used to
work with. She quit. No surprise there.

Q: Why do you think he lost interest
in you?
A: I think he feels threatened by me. A
couple of years ago, I went out and got
a job. I had to, to help pay our son's
college tuition. But I ended up loving
the work. I'm good at it, too, and I
make a lot of money. More than my husband, in fact. He says that it doesn't
bother him, but I'm not so sure.

Q: Do you two fight?
A: We never used to. Maybe we should
have. We kept everything inside, trying
to pretend nothing was wrong. But then
I caught him with that woman. He denied
everything. I accused him of lying, he
accused me of not trusting him. Then, to

punish me, he started telling me I wasn't a good wife and mother. Apparently, he wants me to have a full-time job and make him a three-course dinner every night. I say we both work, so we should both be responsible for the house and the kids.

Q: Name one thing that you love about your husband.

A: Hmmm. (pause) I like watching him talk to his customers about the antiques that he sells. He's so knowledgeable, so passionate. It reminds me of when I first met him.

Q: What would you like to change about him?

A: I'd like him to be more practical, more of a businessman. And I want him to appreciate me. Not just for the woman that I used to be, but for the person I am now.

Q: Do you think you'll be able to work things out?

A: (sigh) I'd like to. I just don't know if we can.

TRANSCRIPT OF INTERVIEW #7

Subject: male, age 50, married, antiques dealer

Q: Good evening. This is the Corelli Institute for Sociological Research. Do you have a minute to answer a few questions, sir?
A: I suppose so.

Q: Are you in a relationship?
A: (pause) I didn't know these questions were going to be so personal.

Q: I'm sorry, but if you want to be in the running for our fabulous seven-day, six-night trip to Italy, you have to answer the questions.
A: Well . . . no.

Q: No, you won't answer the questions, or no, you're not in a relationship?
A: (pause) My wife and I are separated.

Q: And there are no other relationships in the picture?
A: No! My wife thinks so, but she's wrong.

Q: How so?
A: She saw me hugging another woman. But it wasn't what it looked like. The woman was a business associate. A friend of the family, for heaven's sake. She hugged me because I'd just found out that my

business had lost money for the third
year in a row.

Q: Your wife doesn't trust you?
A: She used to. Once upon a time, she
thought the sun rose in my eyes. (laughter) That was back when we were both
young and stupid.

Q: What first attracted you to her?
A: She laughed at my jokes. But it was
more than that. She listened to me.
Really listened. She made me feel that
my dreams were worthwhile. When I married her, I was certain that together,
we could take on the world.

Q: And that changed?
A: I got a hard dose of reality when my
first son was born. I had to work two
jobs so my wife could stay home with
him. But after a lot of sweat and sacri-
fice, I was finally able to open my own
business. Then we had two more children,
and I had to work harder and harder to
support the family.

Q: Why didn't your wife get a job?
A: Neither of us wanted her to--we both
believed the kids should have at least
one full-time parent. (pause) Look, what
does this have to do with male-female
relationships?

Q: That's what I'm trying to find out. What went wrong with your marriage?

A: I failed, that's what went wrong. My first son was applying to college, and we needed more money. I couldn't make enough, so my wife had to get a job to keep us afloat.

Q: And that caused problems.

A: Not at first, when she was working part-time. But then she decided to get her real estate license. Suddenly, she was out at night, working on the week-ends. It was like . . . like she had something to prove. In two years' time, she was earning more than I was.

Q: And that bothered you?

A: Yes . . . No . . . I mean, I was proud of her. And we needed the money. But little by little I felt like I was losing her. She was constantly working, staying out late. She stopped eating dinner with the family, stopped volun-teering at the kids' school. (pause) She stopped listening to me.

Q: And then?

A: She saw me with that woman, and she flipped. At first I was glad. I thought, I've scared her. She'll cut back on her work and try to woo me back. Instead, it was exactly the opposite. She threw herself completely into her job. She was never at home, and when she was, we fought. It got worse and worse until I finally moved out.

Q: Name one thing that you love about your wife.

A: (pause) She's great with the kids. And I love her enthusiasm. When she's excited about something, you can't help but get excited, too. Oh, and she's got a smile that could melt the polar ice caps. I miss it, I really do. I miss her. She doesn't realize how much I need her.

Q: Name one thing you'd change about your wife.

A: I wish she'd slow down. (pause) You know what I would do if I won that trip to Italy? I'd surprise her with it. I'd just drive her to the airport and whisk her on that plane before she knew what was happening. Italy's a pretty romantic place, you know. Maybe in an atmosphere like that, without all the everyday stuff to distract us, we could reconnect. At least I'd like to try.

Chapter Sixteen

Bridgette lay in bed with her eyes wide open. Thoughts were bouncing around inside her head like kernels of popcorn in a microwave.

"They still love each other," she whispered. "I know they do."

She replayed the tapes in her mind for at least the hundredth time that night. "I want him to appreciate me," she heard Mom saying.

"She doesn't realize how much I need her," Dad seemed to answer.

Mom and Dad had said those things to someone they'd thought was a total stranger. So why couldn't they say them to each other? *I have to help them,* Bridgette thought desperately.

But how? Get Mom and Dad together in a room and turn on the tape recorder? Oh, sure. They'd probably stomp out the instant they realized what was going on. Then they'd stomp back in and ground Bridgette until her eighteenth birthday.

Oh, why does it all have to be so complicated? she wondered. She thought about the romance movies she'd watched with Brendan. They made love seem so simple. A couple of twists, a few little turns, but always a happy ending. Why couldn't real life work the same way?

She knew the answer. When you tried to live your own life like a movie, you ended up falling in a cow patty. Or having a bucket of water dumped on your head. Or standing by, helpless and confused, while your formerly happy little nuclear family exploded into a billion pieces.

Bridgette groaned. The sun was coming up and she still didn't have a clue what to do about her parents. She grabbed her head, willing the corn-kernel thoughts to form themselves into some sort of reasonable plan. But they just kept on popping, crazy and out of control.

"Hey, Bridgette," Jake Farley called as she stepped off the school bus the next morning, "I hear your Secret Admirer arrived with a big splash last night."

Bridgette flinched. Against all odds, she had hoped that maybe—just maybe—Aaron would have kept the events of last night to himself. Now her hope collapsed like a soap bubble under a toddler's shoe.

Lowering her head, she walked quickly toward the building. But Todd Lutz stepped in front of her. "Don't be a wet blanket, Bridgette," he said. "Tell us what happened."

"Poor Bridgette," Roger Singleton sneered. "I think she's still feeling a little water-logged."

"Love will do that to you," Jake chuckled. "Isn't that right, Bridgette?"

"Oh, look," Todd announced suddenly, "here comes Bridgette's Secret Admirer!"

Bridgette looked up to see Aaron strolling across the sidewalk. "Aw, you dried your hair," he said with a disappointed frown. "Too bad, Bridgette. That drowned-rat look really suited you."

The boys laughed, and Bridgette felt her cheeks grow hot. "Leave me alone," she muttered.

"Come on, Bridge," Aaron said, slipping his arm around her waist, "don't tell me you don't love me anymore."

Quickly she pulled away, only to realize that a small crowd had gathered around her. The kids were whispering to each other, spreading the news of her humiliation. She tried to push her way through the giggling onlookers, but Aaron grabbed her arm and dragged her back.

"I know you used to care about me, Bridgette," he insisted. "I've got the love letters to prove it." He pulled one out of his pocket and shook it open. "'Dear Secret Admirer,'" he read, "'I dream of the day we'll meet face to face. Our eyes will connect, our hands will touch, then I'll melt into your arms—'"

"And get a big bucket of water right in the kisser!" Jake shouted.

The crowd burst out laughing. Bridgette wanted to melt into the ground.

Suddenly, she felt a hand tighten over hers, jerking her sideways. She gasped and tensed, but the hand kept pulling her. The crowd parted as she stumbled through it.

"Come on, Bridgette," an urgent voice said in her ear. "This way!"

Vaughn!

Chapter Seventeen

"Let's get out of here," Vaughn said, breaking into a jog. He led Bridgette around to the side of the school.

"In here," he said, opening a door. They stepped into an empty stairwell and sat on the bottom step, trying to catch their breath.

"So," Vaughn said at last, "your Secret Admirer turned out to be a snake in the grass."

She laughed. "A snake in a tree, actually. But getting drenched wasn't half as bad as knowing the entire school is now laughing themselves silly at my expense."

Vaughn nodded. "Believe me, I know what you mean. Do you remember the day I told you that

Aaron was bragging to his friends about how you were going to write his report for him? Well, he figured out that I was the one who tipped you off. So the next day, in the locker room after P.E., he and his buddies pulled off my gym shorts and flushed them down the toilet." Vaughn sighed. "I'll never live that one down."

"Oh, Vaughn, I'm sorry."

He shrugged and pulled a pack of gum from his pocket. "I don't know what you saw in Aaron anyway," he said, offering her a stick.

Bridgette popped the gum into her mouth and let the sweet peppermint taste wash over her tongue. "Henry Fonda in *The Lady Eve,*" she said.

He gazed at her quizzically, and she added, "It's a long story."

"I've got time," he said.

The words were barely out of his mouth when the bell rang. They both laughed.

"Maybe later," she said, getting to her feet.

"I'm going to hold you to that," he replied.

When school ended, Vaughn was waiting at Bridgette's locker. "Want to walk over to the pool together?" he asked.

"Sure," she replied. It felt good to be back to their old routine.

As they strolled across the playing fields, Vaughn said, "OK, I'm ready for that long story you were going to tell me."

"Oh, it's ridiculous," she said with an embarrassed laugh. "I'm writing my research paper on true love and . . . well, I thought if I could find love, then I'd really understand what it's all about."

"True love? With *Aaron Shoening?*" Vaughn asked in disbelief.

"I told you it was ridiculous."

They walked on in silence. Then Vaughn said, "A research paper on love, huh? How come that topic?"

"Well," she began slowly, "I guess it all started at the end of the summer . . ."

Before she knew it, Bridgette was telling Vaughn about her parents' fights, her telephone interviews, Trent and Celia's rehearsal dinner, even her disastrous attempts to find the boy of her dreams. Finally, as they reached the pool, she told him about her phone interviews with Mom and Dad.

"Maybe I'm crazy," she said, stopping outside the locker room door, "but I keep thinking that if Mom listened to Dad's interview and he listened to hers, they could straighten things out."

"So why don't you just give them the tapes and make them listen?" Vaughn asked.

"Are you kidding? I can't even get my parents in

the same room together," replied Bridgette.

"Who says they have to be in the same room?"

Bridgette considered that for a moment. She supposed she *could* ask Mom and Dad separately. She wouldn't say what was on the tapes, just tell her parents it was really important. But lately Mom and Dad had been so distracted by other things, she didn't think they'd even listen to her. She could just hear her mother—"Bridgette, I don't have time for this." And her father was so busy worrying about his antiques business, he didn't seem to care about anything else.

"Easier said than done, I'm afraid," Bridgette said to Vaughn.

He frowned thoughtfully and ran his hands through his dark brown hair. "I don't know, Bridge. Sometimes you have to make a bold move. I mean, there's gotta be a way to make them listen."

Bridgette thought it over. Vaughn was right. She needed to find a way to grab her mother and father's attention before they knew what was happening. But how?

Then it came to her. If she could just pull it off . . .

"What are you thinking?" Vaughn asked. "You look like you've got an idea."

"Maybe," she admitted, "but I don't want to jinx it. I'll let you know what happens." Bridgette opened the door to the locker room. Then she turned back to Vaughn.

"What?" he said.

"Nothing. I mean, I just wanted to say thanks."

Vaughn smiled a crooked little smile. "Anytime, Zebra Girl," he said.

Chapter Eighteen

The sky was a pale gray when Bridgette woke up on Saturday morning. Shivering, she slipped out of bed and pulled on her clothes. Then she grabbed the two cassette tapes from her desk and tiptoed into the hallway, pausing a moment to listen to Brendan's soft snoring.

Behind the other bedroom door, she heard Mom roll over and sigh.

Bridgette padded down the stairs and opened the hall closet. In a gym bag on the floor, she found her mom's jogging shoes and her Walkman. Quickly, she opened the Walkman and pulled out the cassette that was in it. It was a book-on-tape called *Starting Over After Divorce.*

Bridgette grimaced and tossed the tape into the back of the closet. Then she replaced it with the cassette of Dad's interview. "Time for your Saturday morning run," she whispered, glancing up toward Mom's room. "Come on, let's burn some calories."

She wiggled into a pair of sneakers, grabbed her coat, and walked out to the garage. On Dad's workbench she found the coffee can that held the family's duplicate keys. She rifled through the can until she found one to Dad's car. Then she wheeled her bike outside and hopped on.

The sky was brightening from gray to blue, and there were streaks of pink on the horizon as she set off down the road.

Thirty minutes later, panting and sweating, she pedaled into the parking lot of the Harvest House Motel. She found Dad's car and unlocked it, certain that at any moment a policeman would appear and arrest her for breaking and entering. But none appeared, so she extracted the tape from his cassette deck and glanced at it. *Jazz Classics.*

At least Dad isn't listening to books about divorce, she thought. She felt hopeful as she popped Mom's interview into the slot.

Dad always went to the bakery on Saturday mornings. "Think Danish and coffee," she said out loud. "You want it, Dad. I know you do."

She closed the car and got back on her bike. A bold move, she thought as she coasted out of the parking lot. It had sounded so reasonable when Vaughn said it. But would it work?

"What's with you?" Brendan asked, sipping his orange juice as he glanced up from an Alfred Hitchcock biography.

Bridgette stopped pacing and gulped down the last of her Pop-Tart. Mom had jogged off down the driveway almost an hour ago. Surely she had listened to Dad's interview by now. So where was she?

"Are you waiting for some boy to call or something?" Brendan asked.

"Don't be stupid."

"Well, I can't think of anything else that would make you so jumpy."

Bridgette dropped another Pop-Tart in the toaster. She wanted desperately to tell Brendan what was going on. But what was the point? He was so lost in his own little world, he probably hadn't even noticed that Dad had moved out.

The sound of a car pulling into the driveway made Bridgette jump. Her chest was thumping as she ran to the front door. When she saw Mom and Dad getting out of Dad's car *together,* her heart took flight. But then she saw their faces—serious and somber. Mom spotted Bridgette and said, "Where's Brendan? We have to talk."

Moments later, they were all assembled in the living room. Bridgette sucked the inside of her cheek so hard it hurt. Dad was looking at her. She tried to read his expression, but all she saw was weariness in his eyes.

"Which one of you thought up the interviews?" her father asked. "And who did you get to ask the questions?"

Bridgette was puzzled. Then she remembered that her voice had been unrecognizable. "I did the interviews myself," she said. "I bought a voice changer at the Electronics Barn, and I put it on the lowest setting possible."

"What are you guys talking about?" Brendan asked, looking confused.

Dad ignored him. "That was you, Bridgette?" he asked with astonishment. Mom looked stunned.

"Well, how else could I find out what was going on?" Bridgette said. "I was desperate. You never tell us anything. All you do is bad-mouth each other."

"OK," Mom said defensively, "I admit we've had a few arguments . . ."

"A few?" Brendan burst out. "You guys are like Michael Douglas and Kathleen Turner in *The War of the Roses!* You argue all the time, and you put us in

146

the middle. Like that whole fiasco on Mom's birthday. What were you guys thinking?"

Bridgette couldn't believe her ears. Brendan *had* been paying attention. She felt like hugging him.

"I think you're exaggerating, Brendan," Mom said.

Dad shook his head sadly. "He's not. That's why I moved out. It was the only way I could think of to stop the fighting."

"But it's *not* the only way," Bridgette insisted. "You heard the tapes, right? Why can't you guys work things out?"

"It's not that simple," Mom said. "You're kids. You don't understand—"

"No one said it was going to be easy," Bridgette shot back, "except Hollywood and the people who write those sappy romance novels. But come on, you guys, don't you think it's worth trying?"

Silence. Had she gone too far? Bridgette held her breath and prayed.

Slowly, Mom turned to Dad. "Dermott, I want things back to the way they used to be."

"So do I, Josie," he said. "But I don't know if that's possible. We've both changed so much." He paused. "But maybe we could work on building something new together. Something we both feel good about."

A tear slid down Mom's cheek. She nodded. "I'm willing to give it a try."

Bridgette wasn't sure if she was going to laugh for joy or burst out crying. Maybe both.

"I think we need some time alone, kids," Dad said.

"Oh, sure," Bridgette said quickly. "No problem. Come on, Brendan, you want to watch a video?"

"Naw," he said. "Let's drive to the bakery. We can grab some doughnuts and, I don't know, hang out."

Bridgette's first impulse was to throw her arms around her brother and smother him with kisses, but she controlled herself. Still, she couldn't stop the grin that was spreading up her cheeks. "Sure," she said as she walked toward the front door, "why not?"

Dear Cupid,

After Mom and Dad listened to the tapes and agreed to talk, I guess I was expecting—hoping, anyway—that their relationship would be instantly transformed. You know, they'd start acting like a couple of newlyweds, and everyone would live happily ever after.

But it hasn't happened. Well, not like I imagined, anyhow. Mom and Dad are going to couples' counseling. They still fight sometimes, but they try not to do it when Brendan and I are around.

Then, last weekend, Dad moved back in. At first, he and Mom were a little too friendly, a little too polite, like they'd forgotten how to act around each other. But now I think they're starting to remember. A couple of days ago I heard them in the kitchen, laughing together. It was a sound I hadn't heard in a long time, and it felt good.

And last night at dinner—yep, we actually ate dinner together, even though it was only microwaved pizza—Mom announced that she's quitting her job. She's not planning on staying home and baking cookies, though. She's going to work for Dad, as his business manager. He'll handle the merchandise, the buying and selling; she'll manage the

money and do what it takes to make the store "com-
petitive with the outlet malls," whatever that means.

Mom also made some comment about how her goal
was to keep Dad as far away from bankruptcy lawyers
as possible. That made me think of the message I'd
heard on our answering machine last month, when Dad
said he was stopping by the lawyer's office. So I asked
Mom and Dad about it, and sure enough, he was meeting with a bankruptcy lawyer, not a divorce attorney!

But the best news of all is that my parents seem
really excited and happy. At one point, while they
were explaining things to us, Mom reached over and
squeezed Dad's hand. Dad turned to her and smiled. It
made me feel all warm inside, like I'd swallowed a ray
of sunshine.

While all this has been going on, Cupid, I've been
finishing up my research paper. I've reread all my notes,
glanced over the letters I've written to you, and listened again to all the interviews. And you know what
I've learned?

Nothing.

Well, not nothing, exactly. I've learned that there's
a big difference between real love and the Hollywood
happily-ever-after kind. I haven't got it all figured out
yet, but believe it or not, that's just fine with me—
for now, anyway.

Come to think of it, there's another thing I learned. I started my research thinking it would help me find a boyfriend. But what I discovered was that I'd rather have Vaughn Steinhauser as a friend ANY day, than one of those other guys as a boyfriend.

He's funny and smart and easy to talk to. And now I'm remembering how he asked me to the Halloween Dance, not at the last minute like he couldn't get anyone else to go with him, but weeks ago, when news of the dance was first announced.

And I'm wondering if he's asked anyone else. Because suddenly, Cupid, I can't think of anyone I'd rather go with.

Meet the Author

Francess Lantz

Then

Now

As a girl growing up in Bucks County, Pennsylvania, Francess Lantz loved to write stories and dreamed of someday moving to California. Later, she switched to songwriting and spent several years trying (unsuccessfully) to become a rock star. Eventually, however, she rediscovered her passion for books. She became a children's librarian and began writing again. Thirty books later, she's still at it. And she lives four blocks from the beach, in Santa Barbara, California, with her son and their dog, Badger. Fran is also the author of *Stepsister from Planet Weird,* which was made into a movie for the Disney Channel.